SLAVE TO LOVE

T0105345

Also edited by Alison Tyler

SLAVE TO LOVE

EROTIC STORIES OF BONDAGE AND DESIRE

EDITED BY
ALISON TYLER

FOREWORD BY
MISTRESS KAY

CLEIS
PRESS

Copyright © 2006, 2011 by Alison Tyler.

All rights reserved. Except for brief passages quoted in newspaper, magazine, radio, or television reviews, no part of this book may be reproduced in any form or by any means, electronic or mechanical, including photocopying or recording, or by information storage or retrieval system, without permission in writing from the publisher.

Published in the United States by Cleis Press, Inc., 2246 Sixth Street, Berkeley, California 94710.

Printed in the United States.
Cover design: Scott Idleman/Blink
Cover photograph: Roman Kasperski
Text design: Frank Wiedemann
Cleis Press logo art: Juana Alicia
10 9 8 7 6 5 4 3 2 1

"Master of Technology" by Vanessa Evans originally appeared as "Training Session" in *Penthouse Variations Magazine* and is reprinted by permission, © 2005, General Media Communications, Inc. All rights reserved.

Trade paper ISBN: 978-1-57344-650-1
E-book ISBN: 978-1-57344-671-6

For SAM

Contents

FOREWORD

Mistress Kay

I love that look in his eyes. When he looks back at me, with reverence in his eyes, like all that matters in this moment is his submission to me. With his arms tied closely against his back as he leans forward on his hands and knees, his butt is exposed to the flogger I'm about to subject his flesh to. A warm, healthy glow on his naked body, a slight quiver in his body when I take a short break to make the longing flood throughout his body before laying the flogger into his skin again.

There's something powerful about knowing you hold an entire person's life in your hands—and they trust you to have it. After all, with the rope tied tightly, a blindfold over their eyes, and a gag in their mouth, you could just walk out and leave them to fend for themselves. But you don't. That's what makes being bound so erotic. There's something about turning over your life to another person, accepting when they push you to your body's limit, making you cry out or beg, that inherently makes erotic restraint so sexy.

Slave to Love really embodies that total feeling of surrender—and the total feeling of power that comes with it. Even if you're just curious and have never felt the cold metal of handcuffs or the sensual restraint of a silk scarf, this collection of stories will throw you into the mindset of the Dominants and submissives who enjoy kink.

In one of my favorite stories, "Unlike the Others" by Xavier Acton, a male visits a professional Dominatrix—she never expected to find herself aroused by the feeling of this submissive male on her lap, but she soon finds herself enjoying it for more than the pay. In another one of my favorites, "Sonnet" by Cate Robertson, I found myself turned on by the complete submission that the girl gives her Master—one that we get the privilege of observing through the story.

Along with the arousal you'll feel from the stories, each one of the tales in this collection is going to give you a close-up look into the erotic power exchange that goes along with restraint. Each tale provides a variety of realistic but unique settings that grip you, the reader, into the action. You find yourself feeling the suspense the submissive feels while she waits for the slap of a hand to lay across her backside. You will find yourself feeling the strength the Dominant feels while he watches his girl display herself for him.

Alison Tyler has done an amazing job bringing together these tales of erotic slavehood. No matter which story you choose to start your adventure in, you'll want to finish your adventure with the feeling of the cuffs on your own wrists—and that's exactly what an erotic story should do.

Mistress Kay

INTRODUCTION

Alison Tyler

You always remember your first. The first time you were tied down. First time you were bound. Blindfolded. Teased. Tormented. Or the first time you did all those decadent activities to someone else.

I remember the very first time I read about BDSM. It was in a Los Angeles restaurant, at the counter where I sat every day. I'd bought *The Story of O* on the recommendation of a casual acquaintance, and I read the little white-covered tome during my lunch break. Not the whole thing, but enough. Enough to make me curious about the man who'd said this was a book for me. Joshua wasn't a boyfriend, wasn't anyone I'd ever looked at in a sexual way. He was an advertising executive, slick in his black suit and skinny red tie, oily with clients on the phone, most in his element selling space to strangers. But that morning he'd come into the newspaper where we both worked and rather than exchanging bland pleasantries as was our normal custom, he'd told me I'd like the book. Said it casually, the way one might discuss a good movie, a nice place to eat. Something simple. Something safe.

Why I took his advice, I still don't know. We never had that much in common, rarely spoke outside polite greetings of "hello" and "fine weather." But I bought the title that day, and I sat at the counter of Maple Drive at noon, reading. More than reading. Devouring. Consuming. Lunch totally forgotten. When I went back to work in the afternoon, I looked at this ad man in a completely different manner. If Joshua could recommend a book like this, could he sense my multitude of perverse desires, as well? Did he know that I wanted someone to cuff me to a bed, to fuck me in an alley, to make me call him Daddy?

The look in his gray blue eyes made me think that he did.

It was a lesson for me. A first—the first time I understood that there are dominants and submissives, that they find each other out, that they have to.

My goal in putting together *Slave to Love* was to create the same erotically charged emotion in readers that *I* had when I woke up to this world. I wanted to revel in the needs, the urges, the magnetic desires that draw people together. People whose needs magically fit with their partners' desires. People for whom fucking is so much more than two bodies coming together—a complicated meshing of power and rules, of pain and pleasure.

As you'll find, for the authors in this collection, the concept of *Slave to Love* unleashed a wide variety of different themes. Some writers created serious S/M tales of torment, others took a more poetic view of the beauty of bondage. That's not to say there aren't any dungeons here—because there are. Michael Hemmingson exorcises old demons in "Betty's Bottom" at a pay-to-play dungeon in Los Angeles. Jean Roberta discovers her crush has a well-equipped basement room in "Down Below." "Unlike the Others," by Xavier Acton, explores a submissive male and his neophyte domme. And, yes, there are Masters and subs—on fervent display in Cate Robertson's wicked "Sonnet" and C. D. Formetta's tersely written "Everything That You Want": *Franco was born to command, and I was consumed inside by the will to obey him. Together we formed a perfect combination.*

Characters in several of the stories engage in intense 24/7 Dom/sub relationships—for instance, in Vanessa Evans's "Master of Technology," in which a slow to upgrade woman is regularly punished for her backwardness:

I gritted my teeth and waited for the first blow. Of course, Morgan let me wait. He never starts a spanking right away. After stripping my clothes off completely, he always takes his time, making me tremble in anticipation. My whole body tenses, readying itself for the surprising burst of pain to start.

Also included are role-playing stories, featuring lighthearted pony-girl porn, as described delightfully in Michelle Houston's "Cowboy's Dungeon," or through a more taboo, shadowy lens, as in Erica Dumas's rape fantasy, "Without Mercy":

You promised to take me without mercy. I begged you for it, and now you're going to do it. And I'm scared. I'm so incredibly scared. I'm scared of giving in, I'm scared of resisting. I want it, and I've wanted it forever. But I'm scared.

And then there are stories that capture that first-time awakening, as in Rachel Kramer Bussel's aptly named "The Discovery," in which a woman finds a box containing her lover's collection of S/M porn:

As I pawed through the box, unearthing images I'd never even come close to imagining, what surprised me the most wasn't that Brian, my Brian, owned and obviously valued these items enough to take them with him and keep them hidden, but how hot they were making me.

Or there's Saskia Walker's well-crafted "Watching Lois Perform," in which the main character is taunted by the clever Jack until he admits what she hasn't yet understood—"I'm a slave to this as much as you are."

As am I. A slave to the concept of power play. A slave to the talent of the authors in this collection. A slave to the deliriously sexy world of bondage and boundaries and breaking the barriers.

Alison Tyler

WATCHING
LOIS PERFORM

Saskia Walker

T rust me, Lois." Jack's arm shot out, blocking the doorway
to her office. "I know what you need." His shirt sleeve was
rolled up, revealing a strong forearm dusted with black hair, his
fist sure and large against the door frame. Halted in her steps,
she took a deep breath. Her glance moved to meet his. "Trust
me, Jack, you don't." Steeling herself, she pushed his arm aside,
ignoring his knowing look, ignoring those dark eyes filled with
suggestion and the tangible wall of testosterone he exuded.

She headed for her desk, her stiletto heels clicking over the
polished wood floor. The skin on her back prickled with awareness, awareness brought about by his presence. He'd done it
again. He'd made her curious, responsive. She didn't take any
nonsense from the men she worked with, but Jack Fulton had
unsettled her. Counting to five, she put her laptop down on the
desk and turned to face him, ready to challenge his comment.
The door was ajar, the space empty. He was gone.

She shook her head. "Typical." Grabbing her bag and coat, she left the building.

The pavement outside was growing crowded with commuters; the Friday evening London rush hour was under way. She stepped into the crush, leaving the office behind, hurrying to the tube station and descending the escalator at a pace. The display board told her it was four minutes until her train was due. She strode up and down the platform, her body wired. She was always like this after delivering a successful presentation. It had gone well, and she'd easily dealt with the put-downs issued by the men who defied her female power. She thrived on her success, but now she longed to throw off her city suit and heels.

The crowd thickened on the platform behind her, noisy and restless. Wind funneled down the tunnel, a distant train rumbled. She glanced across the tracks. Her breath caught in her throat when she saw Jack standing opposite her, still as a predator about to pounce. A barely perceptible smile lifted the corners of his mouth. Even across the rail tracks she could see the intense look in his eyes.

She swallowed. What was it about Jack Fulton? The way he looked at her did powerful things to her, sexual things. They'd worked together for just a few months, but he was one of the few men who didn't challenge her. Instead he sat back with a secret smile, watching as she defended herself at board meetings, where she proved over and again that she had earned her right to be in this male-dominated world. But it was more than that. His dark sexuality was evident in the way he carried himself and the way he scrutinized her. He made her self-aware in the extreme, her underwear soon growing damp when his gaze followed her with that knowing look in his eyes. *The knowing look he had on right now.*

He inclined his head in greeting. She nodded back and then

glanced away, fidgeting with the strap of her shoulder bag. One minute until her train would arrive. His earlier comment echoed through her mind: *I know what you need.* Her curiosity was growing. Her instant denial had been because of the controversy at the meeting, where she'd been giving the research stats for a proposal to change power source in the company's major manufacturing plant. Men were always telling her they knew better than her, even though it was her field of expertise. As soon as she'd rebuffed Jack's comment about knowing what she needed, she'd realized he meant something other than work. Something more intimate. She wanted to know more. And he'd gone.

Glancing back, she saw that his train was approaching. He never took his eyes off her. She craned her neck when her view was obscured by the moving carriages. The shift of the crowd into the train made it impossible to pick him out. Then it was gone. The platform was empty. She stared at the place where he had stood until her train pulled in. She moved to the far side of the carriage, where she could stand out her journey, and turned on her heel just in time to see Jack close in behind her.

"Your place it is then." His eyes glittered with anticipation, with certainty.

Her heart thudded in her chest. Her lips parted, but this time no retort emerged. Between her thighs, a pulse throbbed with need. She closed her mouth, snatching at the overhead handhold for support.

His smile was triumphant.

Later, in her flat, he threw her by rejecting a comfortable, relaxed seat on the sofa. Instead he pulled out a dining chair, indicating that she do the same and sit facing him.

He'd teased her all the way home, innuendo in his every word, keeping her wired. And now, despite the fact they were in her home, he took charge immediately. Not in an aggressive way, but with a relaxed sense of surety that was disarming. She put her wineglass down on the table and took her seat, noting how exposed the setup made her feel.

He lounged back over his chair, one leg folded, his ankle resting on the opposite knee, his hand loosely on the juncture. His looks were rugged but suave. He was dangerously attractive.

She tried to look as relaxed as he appeared, but she was far from it.

"I enjoyed watching you deal with that moron Laybourne at today's meeting."

She gave a breathy laugh, releasing some of the tension he had aroused in her. "He's just an arrogant little prick with very little real knowledge."

"You're so right." He gave a deep and genuine laugh. "He's jealous of your abilities though, and he's lusting after your body. The two vying motivations confuse him. Lust for a competitor can screw with a guy's mind." He looked at her with deliberation.

Her heart raced. "It can?"

"If he lets it." His gaze moved over her body, slowly.

"And are you jealous of my skills?" She crossed her legs high on the thigh, crushing the pounding pulse in her clit.

"No, I admire them immensely. I'm not threatened by you."

Then for a moment silence hung heavy in the atmosphere.

He raised one eyebrow. "I notice you didn't ask if I lusted after you."

"I don't think you came here with the sole purpose of analyzing today's meeting."

He tipped his glass at her. "Indeed. And you did let me come home with you."

She couldn't deny it. "So I did."

Silent acknowledgment raced between them. *We are going to fuck.*

He took a sip of his wine, eyeing her as she crossed and uncrossed her legs.

"It's not easy for you, is it? Blonde, pretty, extraordinarily intelligent."

Something akin to relief hit her. "No, it isn't." She smiled, genuinely appreciating his words. He really had been observing her.

"What do you usually do, when you bring a man home for sex?" He said it as if he was discussing the weather, and glanced around the open-plan living area, as if the furniture could tell tales.

"Oh, fast, dirty sex, nothing prolonged in terms of involvement. I don't have time." She pushed her heavy hair back from her face, watching for his response. It was the truth. What would he think of her?

"That doesn't surprise me."

"Really?"

"Perhaps you should make time."

"Perhaps I should." *Where was he going with this?*

"How many times do you reach orgasm, when you have 'fast, dirty sex'? "

It felt as if the temperature had risen dramatically. "That's a rather intimate question."

"I mean to be intimate with you, Lois."

He wasn't kidding. His provocative questioning had her entire skin prickling. "Once, mostly," she replied eventually.

He nodded. "I'd like to see you come more than once. You deserve better than that."

If he'd wanted to grab her attention, he'd certainly found the way. Up until that moment she could have turned away, asked him to leave. Not now. Not anymore.

"There's a determination about you that fascinates me," he continued. "You stalk after everything. If we were living in a primitive world, you would be a powerful huntress."

She smiled at the image, loving it. "Very amusing, but what's your point?"

"My point is that even powerful women can learn by pacing themselves." He ran one finger around the rim of his wineglass. "You might benefit from restraint."

Her sex clenched. The nape of her neck felt damp. "You're suggesting bondage?" She let her gaze wander over his body: bulky with muscle, his expensive clothing barely concealed his obvious strength. Being under him would be quite something.

He shook his head. "No. I'm talking about a different kind of restraint altogether. *Willpower.* I enjoy seeing you battle with your energies, using and controlling your power in the workplace. Whether it's in the boardroom or elsewhere, your desires are only just harnessed. You're a powerful woman, but it's as if you're always on the edge of losing control. And that is such a turn-on."

Breathing had become difficult. More than that, his words about willpower struck a note with her, and she recognized herself in what he said. She had never thought about it that way, but *yes.* He was right.

He smiled and it was filled with dangerous charm. "I'm enjoying watching you now; you're racked with sexual tension. I can almost touch it." He moved his hand, as if he was touching her from where he sat. "Your eyes are dilated, slightly glazed. Your body is restless, your movements self-conscious, jumpy; your skin is flushed. Your nipples are hard."

She took a gulp of wine. The way he described her was sending her cunt into overdrive.

He loosened his tie. "You've been squirming on that seat for the last five minutes. I'd put money on your underwear being very, very damp."

Her skin raced with sensation, the thrill of his words touching her every inch of skin, inside and out. She wanted to fuck. *Now.* But he was making her sit there and listen, controlling her with his intimate, knowing words.

His glance dropped to her cleavage. She realized her fingers were toying with the button there. She clutched it tight, stilling her hand, and bit her lip.

"Be careful, you'll draw blood."

He didn't miss a thing.

"How wet are you, Lois?"

She squirmed on her chair, desperate for contact, her eyes closing as she replied. "Wet, very wet." She stifled a whimper.

Silence hung heavy between them again while she looked up at him for his response. He was still as a bird of prey, his chin resting on one hand. A large bulge showed in his expensive Armani pants. She wanted it badly, wanted it inside her where her body was begging to be filled.

He lifted one finger, gesturing at her crotch. "Open your legs, show me."

Swearing under her breath, she followed his instruction, dragging her short skirt up and over her hips, her eyes never leaving his. As she opened her legs, pivoting out on her stacked heels, his eyes darkened.

"Oh yes, you are wet." His lips remained apart as he stared at her. She sensed his breathing had grown quicker. "Touch yourself, through your panties," he instructed.

She rested her hand over her pussy and groaned aloud. Her clit leapt, her hips wriggling into her hand for more.

"Enough." He smiled. "Stand and take your underwear off."

Her heart thudded so hard she thought she might crack. She took a deep breath and stood up, rested her thumbs in the lacy waistband and paused.

With one finger, he gestured downward.

She rolled them over her hip bones, growling quietly when she found herself exposed under his gaze. Dropping the panties to the floor, she stepped out of them. Her skirt was wedged around her waist, her pussy exposed. She rested her hands on her hips in an attempt to feel less awkward.

"How delicious. I can see your clit poking out. It's very swollen, isn't it?"

She nodded, her feet shuffling, her face on fire.

He gestured at her abandoned panties. "Pick them up and bring them here."

His instruction hit her like a left hook. He wanted her damp underwear. She steadied herself. Bending to snatch them up, she looked at the floor, counted to five. *He also wanted her to move closer.* Standing, barely in touch with her equilibrium, she swayed on her heels. When she stepped forward, she had the panties clutched against her chest.

He gestured with his hand.

She held them out.

He leaned forward, took the wispy garment. Slowly, he opened the crotch out, holding it up to the light. "Poor Lois, you were finding this hard, weren't you?" A damp patch reminiscent of a Rorschach inkblot spanned the fabric. He breathed in appreciatively, his eyelids lowering. "Delicious."

A combination of embarrassment and nagging lust burned her up inside. Her juices were now marking the insides of her thighs. "Do you get off on making women hot," she blurted, "and then leaving them hanging?"

He rested the panties on the table, next to his wineglass, and put his hand over the bulge in his pants. "I'm a slave to this as much as you are."

"Hardly." He was so controlled. She felt as if she was about to lose it and beg. *Was that what he wanted her to do?*

He moved his hand, unzipping his pants and letting his cock spring free. Moisture dribbled from its tip. With one hand, he rode it up and down, slowly and deliberately, watching her reaction. It was long and thick, a prize specimen, and it was as ready for action as she was. When she glanced back up at his face, she saw it all; saw a mirror of where she was at, wrestling with her inner desires, barely controlling them.

"Hard, isn't it?" His mouth moved in an ironic smile.

"Please. Jack, please?" Her hand had found its way into her pussy.

He watched her hand moving. "What is it that you want?"

"That." She nodded down at his cock, her hand latched over her clit, pressing and squeezing. "Inside me."

"Show me how much you want it."

She stared at him, panting with need, then dropped to a crouch, moving in between his knees to kneel at his feet. She opened her shirt, pulled the cups of her bra down so that her tits pushed out. She plucked at her rigid nipples. "I want it so much," she whispered, looking up at him pleadingly. She licked his cock from where his fist was braced around its base up to the tip and over.

His eyes gleamed with pleasure, his lips parted.

She took the swollen head into her mouth, riding it against the roof of her mouth. When he groaned, she took him deeper, rising and falling, sucking him hard. His hand loosened, his balls rode high. She drew back.

He looked down at her, his eyes glazed. Still he made no move. Her hips swung behind her, her arse in the air, her cunt begging to be filled. "Please, please fuck me. Jack, I'm dying for you to fuck me."

It was as if she'd tripped a switch. Undoing his belt, he stood up, shoving his pants and jockeys to his ankles. He hauled her to her feet, kissed her fiercely, his tongue claiming her lips, her mouth. Between them, one hand moved on his cock, the other stroked her pussy, squeezing it in his hand, sending her clit wild. She whimpered, entirely locked to his actions.

He grabbed her by the shoulders and turned her round, bending her over the dining table, pressing her down onto it, his hands roaming over her exposed buttocks as if, suddenly, he couldn't get enough of it. He kneaded her flesh, hauling her buttocks apart, his cock nudging into her swollen pussy. He grunted with primitive pleasure when her hungry cunt quickly gave way, sucking him in. He bent over her, sliding in, filling her to the hilt.

"Oh, yes." She shuddered with sensation, her hands clawing for the far edge of the table.

"Good?" he murmured against her back. When she moaned agreement, he thrust again, crushing her cervix, circling his hips as if he was testing her for ripeness. "You're so swollen, so sensitive; your cunt is like a hot fist on my cock."

He wasn't kidding. She was already close to coming.

He thrust hard. "Wasn't that worth waiting for?"

She nodded again, awash with sensation, her thighs spreading, her belly flat to the table.

"Ready to be well and truly fucked?"

She opened her mouth to retort, to say she thought she was being fucked already, then she noticed the extent of the tension at her back, like a loaded gun. *He hasn't even started.* She bit her lip, braced her arms, and nodded, her head hanging down.

With the precision of a well-oiled machine, he started to

move, grinding into her, holding her hips as he drove his cock in and out. She pressed back, meeting each thrust with a low cry, pleasure spilling from her core. He filled her completely. She felt wild, yet tethered. She came fast and hot, her cunt in spasm.

"Nice one; feels good, Lois," he panted. "Ready for more?" He stroked her hair, but he didn't break his stride.

She was his, a rag doll to his will, her body riding the table as he fucked her. Her inner thighs were slick with juices. Her feet were off the floor, heels in the air. Her tits and clit were crushed onto the table, fast growing painful with the push and shove on the hard surface.

And then he thrust harder, swearing when he felt the hot clutch of her body on his. His fists grabbed at her buttocks, manhandling her back against his hips, anchoring her on his cock. He was so deep, wedged against her cervix; she felt his cock grow larger still. It lurched, spurting. She wriggled and flexed, on the verge of coming again. He squeezed her buttocks, as if milking himself off with her body. Acute sensation roared through her, spiraling out until every part of her was vibrating. She gave a long, low moan, her body convulsing.

Against her back, Jack breathed hard. She put her hand over his where it rested on her hip, gratitude welling inside her. She'd never had it this hot before, she'd never taken the time.

He reached for her and kissed her cheek, lifting her and sliding her to her feet, supporting her in his arms. "I'm not done with you yet, Lois. I want to see you perform some more."

She gave a breathy laugh, leaning back against him. "Is that a threat or a promise?"

"Consider it a bit of both."

At the end of her presentation, Lois turned to the gathering and smiled, ready to take questions. Most of the board nodded in

agreement. Tim Laybourne rapped his pen on the table, swivel-
ing his gangly head from side to side as he raised the pen in the
air to make a point.

Here we go, let's see if Jack's right. She leaned forward
and put both hands on the table, flashing her cleavage at him.
"Tim, you had a question?" She glanced past him, at Jack, who
winked.

Tim coughed uncomfortably, flushing from the top of his
collar to the roots of his hair. "I remain unconvinced about the
financing of this project." He didn't even sound convinced of his
own words. Jack was right; he had the hots, severely.

She eased onto the table, facing in his direction and resting
on one hip, her short skirt growing even shorter. She lifted the
finance sheet. "The figures don't make sense?" She gave him a
gently enquiring smile.

Laybourne stared at her thigh, open mouthed and speechless.

"If I might interject?" It was Jack and his expression indicat-
ed his restrained humor. "Why don't you just run through that
last part again? I'd certainly appreciate a repeat performance."
He lifted one eyebrow suggestively.

The tone of his voice and the way he looked at her assured
her he wasn't just talking about a run-through on the sums. He
reached for her again, invisibly nurturing her strengths. She'd
always thrived on her role in the workplace, but under his
knowing gaze she reveled in it. Since their encounter the week
before, everything he'd said to her at work had been laden with
suggestion of the sexual kind, keeping their affair on rapid sim-
mer. And right now the tug of his call pulled on her, from cunt
to mouth. She was salivating for more of what he'd given her.

"Of course not, Jack. I'm quite sure it would benefit everybody involved."

Jack nodded, his eyes gleaming with affirmation. Then he sat back in his chair and watched Lois perform, just like he would watch her perform again that night, with measured willpower and the perfect level of restraint, leading to the ultimate mutual reward.

PIERCE ME

Shanna Germain

'd wanted one forever, but the truth was I was chickenshit. Afraid of infection, afraid of pointy things, afraid of needles, and afraid of pain. Not a good combination if, like me, you'd been hankering for a piercing. And, of course, like with everything else I did, I didn't want to start small. No earlobes. No navel. No nose, thank you very much. My dream was bigger than that.

"Why don't you just try your ears first?" Cal asked me when I brought it up—again. We were walking down Hawthorne Avenue, hand in hand, watching the shoppers. A young woman went by, a large sparkling ring in her eyebrow. It looked cool, and she seemed happy with it, but that wasn't what I wanted either.

"I don't want to do my ears." I was trying not to pout about it. It was my own issue. Cal, bless his heart, couldn't do anything to alleviate my love/hate relationship with sticking something metal through my body parts.

"Look," Cal said. "It's a sign." And it was, literally, a sign. But it was also, as he meant it, a *sign*. A big white A-board with black

letters: *Get Your Titties Pierced! Two for One!* I swear I felt it in
my nipples, that sign, like they knew what I was reading.

"We can each take one," I said. I was laughing, of course.
Joking.

Cal wrapped his big hand tighter around mine. His wedding
ring dug into the back of my knuckle as he turned toward the
store and pulled me with him.

"Great," he said.

I let him pull me a few steps before I reached out and grabbed
a handful of his red ponytail. Not hard or anything, just enough
to get him to stop and turn toward me.

"Great, what?" I asked.

Cal had his eyebrow raised the way he does, and there was
something in those tea green eyes of his. I wouldn't say a twin-
kle—more of a scary little point of light, like the ones that lead
people astray through the woods in fairy stories.

"I'm tired of listening to you saying how much you want
this," he said. "Let's just do it. Together. You and me."

I didn't want to think about what he was saying, the way
it was making my belly drop and roll. I stared at the red scruff
around his chin, the two-day beard he always grew on the weekends. Most people thought Cal was hard-core, some kind of reb-
el, when they first met him; I think it's the ponytail and the way
his lips kind of scowl downward, without him even realizing it.
But he's a softie. No tattoos and only one piercing—in his ear—
from his senior year of high school. If you know where to look,
you can almost pick out the healed-over hole tucked into the
constellation of freckles on his earlobe. Now he seemed to be offering himself up to me, but I wanted to be sure.

"Do what?" I asked.

Cal looked at my nipples, already standing out through my
T-shirt, and gave a little thrust with his chin toward the sign.

"Don't be dense on purpose," he said.

And then he waited. I stared at the closed-up hole in his ear-lobe. I crossed my arms over my chest—I don't have much in the way of boobs, but I'm not afraid to admit that I've got pretty damn amazing nipples. Red as raspberries and about as big, especially when I'm turned on. And sensitive? Oh, Jesus.

It was the sensitive part that got me moving again. I pushed Cal away from the store with my hip, almost knocking him into another young woman coming out of the shop. While Cal apologized for me, I tried not to look at her boobs—did she just have her nipples done? Would you be able to tell?

Cal turned back toward me. "Listen—"

I put my hand on his arm, on that little triceps muscle that I love.

"I know you're joking," I said. "So I'm totally not even going to get into it."

"Okay," he said. "But there's something you should know." And then he started walking away, away from the store, away from me.

I reached out and grabbed the belt loop of his jeans, tried to get him to stop walking.

"What?" I said.

"It's a secret," he said, still not looking at me.

"Tell me," I said.

Cal turned and put one hand on my hip, just in front of the curve of my ass. Through my skirt, his fingers were sun warmed and firm. Then he leaned down, his lips just kissing the edges of my lips.

"It's only thirty bucks," he whispered.

I wrapped my fingers through his belt loop again, keeping him close to me.

"How do you know that?" I asked. The sign hadn't said anything about the price.

When Cal grins the way he was now, I know I'm in trouble. One side of his mouth opens up a little, showing off his wide front teeth. And he's got these little laugh lines that curve around the spot where his top and bottom lip meet. I call it his "So, uh" grin, because it usually ends with him saying, "So, uh...." The end of that sentence has led us everywhere from a canoe trip down a Costa Rican river to an entirely different kind of paddle party at the next town over.

He tried to shrug it off, but I kept a tight handle on his belt loop.

"You're serious, aren't you?"

"I might be."

I tried to imagine it—the sharpness of a needle puncturing my already sensitive nipple. It still gave me the shivers—but there was something else too, something that started a slow drumbeat between my thighs. And the thought of Cal getting his nipple pierced too, the fact that it would be for me and only me...

I took a deep breath, let it out slow. My head was spinning a bit. The drum kept its steady rhythm between my legs.

"Okay," I said.

Cal moved so fast, he didn't even wait for the word to finish coming out of my mouth before he took my hand and pulled me inside the store.

The dark-haired woman who met us at the door had a tiny jewel in the skin just above her top lip, and another in her nose. Her smile was cool and professional. In fact, the whole place was more professional than I'd expected. A kind of professional-funky combination that smelled slightly of incense, slightly of alcohol.

"Hi," she said. "I'm Trisha."

She kind of looked at Cal like she knew him, which made me

nervous. Had he been planning this? He was looking into the glass counter so I couldn't see his eyes to get a read on him.

He pointed with his finger on the glass.

"Those bars," he said. "One for each of us. Smaller for her." He said it so quickly, with so much conviction that I wondered how much thought he'd already given to this, how much time he'd spent on it.

Trisha pulled on gloves and reached into the case for the silver bars. She put both of them into her gloved palm. Mine was small and slightly curved, with little blue jewels at both ends. Cal's was thick all the way through, straight and solid, capped off by silver balls.

"Yes?" Trisha asked.

I imagined how that blue would look in my nipple, how it would match my eyes, how it would feel when Cal put his teeth over it, twisted just a little. And then I surprised myself—and I think Cal too—by matching his "yes."

"Great," Trisha said. "C'mon back."

She led us to a small back room that looked like a doctor's office, with one cot, a counter full of supplies and a chair in the corner.

"Ladies first," Trisha said. And I was glad she did. I knew if I watched Cal go first, I would totally chicken out. I sat myself up on the paper-covered table, lifted my shirt off over my shoulders.

"Bra too, honey," Trisha said. She gave a nod at my lacy purple push-up. "Although it sure is a nice one."

As I reached around to unhook the back, I suddenly felt shy. My chin pointed down at my thighs. I held the bra in my lap, fingering the lace and silk cups. Suddenly, I wasn't sure I wanted this. My beautiful, sensitive nipples. What if it hurt too much? What if it scarred me for life?

Cal must have felt something of what I was feeling because he put one finger under my chin and lifted my face to his.

"Look here," he said.

"Okay," I said. I concentrated on the yellow specks that floated in his green eyes. "I'm okay."

And then Trisha brought out the needle. Only it wasn't a needle—it was a bar. Nothing pointy on either end. No machine. No anesthesia. With her gloved hands, Trisha started to open the package.

"What the hell is that?" My palms made wet spots against the lace of the bra.

Trisha held the package toward me, careful not to let anything touch it.

"It's your piercing," she said. "With nipples, you don't need a machine or a point. It just goes right through the skin."

"Fuck," I said. My thighs shook, crinkling the layer of paper on the table beneath me. That bar that had looked so little before now looked huge. A big, wide bar with no pointy end thing was not part of the deal. I wove my fingers deeper into the lace bra, sure I was going to rip the fabric. Even Cal's direct gaze wasn't enough to help me now. I wanted out.

Cal and Trisha waited for me. Cal tried again to hold my eyes with his, then Trisha held the bar in a place where I could look down and see it. Her voice was soft and calming.

"Just imagine it going in," she said. "It's not going to hurt a lot, just a little bit. Just enough to let you feel it."

I felt like a horse being offered a bit for the first time—if I could just stare at it long enough, maybe it wouldn't be so damn scary when they stuck it in.

But it didn't work. My nipples fell flat every time I even began to imagine that thing sliding inside my skin.

Even when Trisha asked which one, and I picked the left, and she ran the cold, wet antiseptic cloth over and over that nipple, even then, I couldn't say yes. Cal was still staring at me—I wanted to make those eyes happy, I wanted to bring the light back in, I wanted my own eyes to reflect the same pain and pleasure and desire that I saw in his.

"I'm sorry," I said. "I just can't."

At first Cal didn't say anything, then, after a moment: "What if I helped you?" His voice was whisper soft, that damn baritone that jolts my clit like a remote vibrator, that gets me to say yes to anything. "I could help her, couldn't I?" he asked. He was speaking to Trisha, but he didn't take his eyes off mine.

Trisha's hands were already unscrewing the balls at each end of the metal bar. She didn't look up from her gloved fingers on the metal.

"You'll need to swing the lock on that door," she said. Something in her voice, in the way she kept right on prepping, told me I wasn't the first to try to back out, that I wasn't the first to need a little persuasion.

Cal swung the deadbolt solid against the lock. When he came back to me, his voice was still in the same down-low, sweet-as-honey tone.

"Okay, baby, put your feet up on this bar here." I did as he said, letting him guide my thighs outward. "Now, look here," he said again.

I looked into those green eyes, tried to fall into them. He put his hands on my thighs and pushed the material of my skirt up as far as it would go. His big hands were warm and firm on the inside of my thigh. When he hit the edge of my underwear I gasped, and slid my eyes toward Trisha.

She held the bar of metal between her pointer finger and thumb.

"Go ahead, honey," she said.

At the same time, Cal slid two fingers inside my underwear.

"Look here," Cal said and I turned my eyes back to him, to the gray hairs that were starting to show through the red just above his ears, to the freckles and the almost-forgotten hole in his lobe.

His fingers pressed against me, forcing me open. I wasn't even wet yet, but I could feel it coming, feel it in the sharp edges of his fingernails, in the rough skin of his knuckles. It was all too fast—I didn't want this piercing, did I? Even with his fingers inside me, I wasn't sure I wanted this.

"Let me," he said, and his voice was growl and gravel.

I opened my thighs as wide as they would go, leaned back on my hands. I looked into his green eyes and let his fingers tuck inside me like I was a book and he was saving his place. It hurt a little, the way it does when you're not ready, burned all the way up my insides, but it was pleasure too. Cal's thumb rocked my clit, soft, side to side, turning the burn into ripples into ache.

Soon he had all four fingers inside me, his thumb on my clit. He put his other hand against my lower back, pushing me forward onto his fingers. I put my hands on his shoulders, feeling the muscles move as he worked me.

Trisha stepped up closer to me. I looked sideways at her, at that bar in her gloved hand, and I lost the rhythm.

When I stopped moving, Cal curled his fingers up inside me, in that C that I love, that makes me feel like I have to pee and come at the same time. I found my rhythm fast, fucking his fingers, leaning forward to press my clit harder against his thumb.

"Are you ready?" Cal asked.

"No, no," I said. "More."

I put my hands back behind me on the paper covering, lifted myself toward his fingers. I didn't want this dumb piercing. I wanted his hand inside me forever, up and down. I wanted his thumb against my clit like this, over and over, harder and harder, until I came. I wanted him to suck my nipples until they ached and sent those little points of pleasure into my belly. And then I wanted to suck him off and go home.

"She's ready," Cal said.

He stopped moving. I would have moved, but Cal held me there, tethered to his fingers inside me, tied to his thumb slowly stroking my clit, all of my body tingling and buzzing. Trisha grabbed my hard nipple with her gloved fingertips and pulled it out away from my body.

"Don't watch," Cal said.

But I couldn't do anything else. The bar came closer and closer to my nipple, Trisha's fingers and her face also closer until I was sure I could feel her breath. It helped if I imagined her reaching out her tongue, nipping me between her teeth, gentle.

And then she was pressing the bar to the side of my skin, pressing it in and through my nipple, and it burned like Cal's hands fucking me, only like it was the first time. That thing inside, that pain and pleasure where before there was nothing.

Cal's thumb was over and over my clit, but I could barely feel it—everything I am was in my chest, in the point of my nipple, in the burn of steel through skin.

"Okay," Trisha said, backing away.

And then I could feel everything: Cal's fingers curling up inside me, the edge of his thumb roughing my clit, my nipple heavy with fire and steel. When the orgasm came, I leaned into it, let it roll like grief, like fear, through the deepest parts of me, let it raze me.

Cal pulled his fingers out of me, slow. I tasted salt at the back of my throat, at the edges of my lips.

"You okay?" Cal asked.

"Fuck." I wasn't sure. My body was all fucked up. My thighs

felt shaky even though I was still sitting down, my insides felt raw. Some part of me wanted to hug Cal and cry on his shoulder, another part of me wanted to slug him. Hadn't he heard me say, "No"? What the fuck had just happened?

And then Cal said, "It's beautiful," and I looked down at my nipple, at the silver bar that peeked from each side of the red skin. It looked like me, but not me. It looked like a better, stronger me. It *was* beautiful—and it was something that I wouldn't have been able to do on my own. I realized Cal had heard me saying no, but he'd also heard me all those times I'd said yes.

Beside me, Trisha snapped her gloves off.

"Everybody okay?" she asked.

This time, Cal and I both nodded.

"Great," she said. She dug a new pair of gloves out of the box on the table. "Because I believe I have one more to do."

Cal's green eyes went a little yellow when she said that. I leaned forward and pressed my palm against the front of his jeans, ran my finger up the edge of his hard-on.

"Don't worry," I said. "I'll help you through it."

UNDER MY THUMB

Thomas S. Roche

Spider was horny when he walked into the hotel room—he was always horny after a gig. But it wasn't like he planned to do anything about it—at least, not right away. After all, he had a 3:00 a.m. "dinner" date with Sierra Verdi from *Darkness Calls* magazine, who, in breaking from her usual reticence the last time he was in town, reviewed Spider's show by saying that "Spider is the only guy in creation besides Billy Bob Thornton whom I would gladly fuck for a dime and a cappuccino."

Spider had a pocket full of dimes, and Daddy's All-Night on Castro had the best espresso drinks of anywhere in town.

He'd already stripped off his sweat-soaked muscle shirt when he hit the lights. For a second, he thought Sierra had jumped the gun on him; in fact, he wondered if maybe she'd waived the cash fee and ordered room service. He'd never actually seen Sierra outside of the photo accompanying her column, and of course hair colors changed as quickly as sexual orientations in the land of rock and roll, so the possibility that Sierra had picked his lock—so to speak—was not dispelled by the fact that it was not a curvy thirtysomething brunette but a slim twentysomething blonde stretched out on the hotel bed wearing only leopard-print underwear and a pair of handcuffs.

But the gag—that *definitely* wasn't Sierra's style.

Spider walked over and sat on the edge of the hotel bed. The chick was young, maybe even younger than midtwenties, and her longish mane of platinum blonde hair lay scattered across the crisp hotel pillows. Her teacup breasts were clutched in a tight push-up bra in pink and silver leopard print with black lace at the top, and her cute little ass was cupped in a matching pair of panties. She lay on her side, twisted slightly so that he could see both ass and tits. Obviously she knew her ass was her best feature, but it received stern competition from the tits, which spilled lushly over the tops of her bra cups.

She was pretty. Her features were delicate, those of a perky rock-and-roll starlet affecting the pierced-and-primped look. She definitely wasn't aping the sexy honorary femme-dyke punk style that Sierra sported. Truth be told, the latter was Spider's preference, but the girl on his bed certainly wasn't in danger of getting kicked out.

The girl's big blue eyes blinked up at him cheerfully, only the oversized gag preventing her from showing a broad smile.

Spider rooted under the bed and found the girl's clothes: skimpy black jean shorts, high boots, and a crop top. Tucked into the shorts was a small key-ring, a packet of lube, and a tiny leather clutch purse. He tossed the lube on the bed, unsnapped the girl's wallet and took out her ID. The ID looked reasonably convincing—she was twenty-two, well within the legal range. Still, he put his hand on the girl's hip, turned her to her side, and unlocked the handcuffs. She wriggled slightly, resisting his attempts to free her and keeping her wrists pressed together behind her back. She whimpered in protest as he unbuckled the gag. It was one of those ring gags like Spider had occasionally seen on bondage websites—allowing full access while preventing effective protest. Though she whined a little, the girl didn't say a word.

She was so petite that it wasn't hard to wrestle her into a sitting position against the hotel headboard, even though she kept trying to rub her ass up against Spider's crotch. She uttered little protests as he did, though, plainly preferring her prone position. But Spider wasn't taking any shit. He turned her around and sat on the bed, opposite her, cross-legged, not even caring that his boots were on the spread.

"Hi," the girl said with a smile. She had a pierced tongue and he could see the faint glint of nipple rings, too, through the pink leopard-print fabric and black lace.

Spider looked at her ID. "Kimberly," he said. "Welcome to my nightmare."

"Ugh," said the girl. "Nobody calls me that. My name's China."

"All right, China. How did you get in the room?"

"Please," said China. "Like wiggling my tits wouldn't get me just about anything I wanted in a hotel like this."

Spider frowned at her.

China looked slightly cowed—she almost blushed.

"I know the bellman," she said. "Please don't get him in trouble."

"Like I have time for that," said Spider. "Listen, I'm going to take a shower."

"I like you dirty."

Spider slapped the girl's thigh, making her jump a little.

"My dear China," he said. "You'll have me clean, if you have me at all. Of course, if you've got second thoughts or the E has started to wear off—"

"I had *one* rum-and-coke," she protested petulantly.

Spider slapped her thigh again.

"Be quiet. If you've got second thoughts, there's the door."

China sat there watching as Spider unbuckled his belt and pulled off his motorcycle boots. He stripped off his stretch jeans as he walked into the bathroom, well aware that China's eyes were burning an invitation into his ass.

The hot water felt good. He heard the doorknob jiggling and was glad he'd locked it. To Spider, showers were one of the few things in the world that were not sexy. He lathered himself up and washed the sweat from his body, brushed his teeth but didn't shave. When he walked out of the bathroom, China was handcuffed and gagged again, spread out on her belly and having discarded the bra and panties. Her legs were spread wide. Her head was turned to the side; she looked up at him with love in her eyes.

He could see that her pussy was both shaved and pierced— four rings through each of her lips. A similar ring glinted from her clit. Her ass was lifted slightly, invitingly revealing her pink asshole between her smooth, well-toned cheeks.

Spider glanced at the bedside clock. It was already two-thirty, and he didn't want to keep Sierra waiting after the months of email flirtation they'd enjoyed. A ten-minute cab ride left just enough time for a quick tryst with a groupie. It's not like he and Sierra had any kind of agreement—on the contrary, in the rock 'n' roll world double-dipping was customary.

He let the white hotel towel drop to the floor, and China's eyes zeroed in on his cock, standing out hard and ready from his body.

"You realize you're about to be used and discarded," said Spider.

"Yes, please," came China's muffled reply from behind the

ring gag. She lifted her ass higher into the air, displaying both it and her pussy for Spider's hungry eyes.

He climbed onto the bed and took hold of China's hair. She wriggled slightly to get into the right position as he guided her face to his cock and slid his cockhead through the ring gag. Her tongue immediately began working along the underside. He would have liked to see what those lips could do, but the sparkle in China's eyes as he fed her his cock was more than enough. He eased his cock deeper into her mouth and with a smooth, expert gesture she opened her throat wide and pushed herself onto him, swallowing him all the way down to his balls.

Her muscles contracted against him as he began to ease his hips back and forth, fucking her throat. He heard a whimper of pleasure deep in China's throat—without a hint of a gag. This was a well-trained groupie, he decided. He ran his hand down to her handcuffed wrists and savored the feeling of having her in bondage, then slowly drew his fingertips up her back, making China's naked body shiver. He grasped her hair tightly and began to fuck China's pretty face.

He could see the moist hint of water in her eyes as his big cock savaged even her well-subdued gag reflex. Leaning heavily over her, Spider reached down and pressed his hand between her legs, feeling that she was even wetter than he'd anticipated. When he touched her clit, her whole body quaked, and she raised her ass high as if to invite him in.

As he fucked China's face, Spider lifted his hand and gave her a hard, merciless spank on her pretty butt. That made her wriggle and whimper as he plumbed her throat. Spider spanked her again and a low moan shivered through his cockhead, trapped in China's breast by the cock filling her throat. He spanked her harder, making her lift her ass to beg for more as her round cheeks pinkened.

God, she looked glorious spread out on the bed like that. Her throat felt so good around his cock, as she bobbed up and down and gasped for air between thrusts. But he knew time was short, and he wanted all there was to have of her.

Spider grasped China's hair firmly and pulled her face off his cock. Her eyes flashed hungrily as she held her lips, forced open by the ring gag, just an inch from his glistening head. Then he grabbed her handcuffed wrists and pulled her up on the bed, forcing her face into a pillow.

Her hips pivoted to accept his cockhead between her pierced pussy lips. She groaned as he entered her, and from the first inch of her cunt Spider realized that he was still underestimating how wet this little groupie was. He drove deep into her, his cockhead striking her cervix with a firm thrust, and a tiny squeal erupted from China's forced-open mouth. He grasped her hair more firmly as he started to fuck her.

Her pussy was tighter than tight. He ground deep into her, feeling the press of her swelling G-spot as his cockhead reached the perfect depth within her. He slipped the thumb of his free hand into her pussy, moistening it as he pulled his cock out for an instant. Then he was back inside her, thrusting deep into her cunt, and another squeal escaped her mouth as he forced his pussy-slick thumb into China's asshole. He seized the little packet of lube he'd taken out of her shorts and ripped it open with his teeth. He drizzled lube between her round cheeks, sliding his thumb in and out to slick up China's asshole. Tight at first, it opened and relaxed as he matched the thrusts of his thumb to the pounding of his cock. China barely seemed to know what was happening as he pulled his thumb and cock out at the same time, positioning his cockhead between her cheeks.

Still using China's hair, he forced her face to the side so he could look into her eyes. As he entered her ass, he saw them go wide at first, then heard her low moan, unmistakably a sound of ecstasy, as he forced his cock slowly further inside. China pushed her ass up against him, meting his thrust and begging him to enter her all the way.

Spider felt China's asshole enveloping his cock. He leaned hard against her body and reached under to feel her clit. It was rock hard, its metal ring standing fully at attention. Spider toyed with it as he took China's ass, each thrust bringing him closer to completion. He leaned down heavily, forcefully turned her face to the side, and pressed his mouth against China's, loving the feel of its softness against her, the fact that her mouth was forced wide open and she could no more resist the hard thrust of his tongue than she could the thrust of his cock up her ass. China began to moan wildly when Spider pulled his mouth off of hers. He pulled the buckle of the gag and tugged it out of her mouth, then kissed her again, hard. As his tongue left her mouth this time, Spider heard her moaning, "Fuck me...fuck my ass...please...harder...fuck my ass harder...come in my ass...."

Spider obliged, pounding China mercilessly as he shoved her ass up into the air. Abandoning her clit, he reached around her and felt the firm, small mounds of her naked breasts, pinching her pierced nipples as he fucked her harder. Then he felt her body go rigid, heard her moans turn to wails, heard her struggle to get out the sobbing words, "I'm coming," as he drove faster and faster into her tight asshole—and he felt the clutch, the rhythmic muscle spasms through China's ass that spelled the intense orgasm of a groupie who'd trained for her moment in the spotlight. The grip of China's no doubt Kegel-enhanced climax drove Spider right over the edge, and he came hard in her ass as she pushed her body up against him, begging for his come.

When he'd finished, he rested there atop her and listened

to the whimpering sounds of China's postorgasmic bliss. He looked at the clock.

He slid out of her, off of her. He found the key chain again and unlocked China's handcuffs, then slapped her once more on the ass, playfully, lightly this time.

"I've got a date," he said.

"I know," said China enigmatically, shooting him a mischievous smile.

Spider went into the bathroom and locked the door again, but this time China didn't try to make her way in. When he came out, the scent of China's body scrubbed from his, he discovered her curled up in bed, the covers pulled over her naked body.

"I'll be back in an hour," said Spider. "I'll probably have company, so please don't be here. I'm calling housekeeping to change the sheets."

"I'll do it," said China, picking up the phone.

Spider listened to her sweet-talking the housekeeping staff as he got dressed. He wondered if the girl was a hotel groupie, too. "Call me a cab, will you?" he asked, and she did, obediently, without hesitation. Spider felt a strange sense of satisfaction about that.

When he was dressed the way he figured Sierra would expect him to be—stretch jeans, tight T-shirt, high boots, and a leather jacket—Spider looked at China, the outline of her body still fetching despite the bulky covers.

"Gone," he said warily. "In an hour. All right?"

She nodded.

"Steal anything, and my goons will track you down and break your legs."

"I love it when you talk dirty," she said.

The cab was waiting downstairs.

* * *

Sierra was already there, sipping an Evian as he slipped into the diner booth. The place was practically empty. She looked even cuter than her picture—dark hair, full features, and thick, kissable lips. She was wearing a tight black dress that revealed the top of her bra with her legendary breasts spilling out. The bra showed black lace, and underneath it pink and silver leopard print. Spider puzzled over that.

"Sierra? It's nice to meet you," he said, shaking her hand. "Sorry I'm late."

"No problem," she said with a knowing smile. "Did you get my gift basket?"

Spider felt a momentary stab of guilt—he hadn't even bothered to check for gift baskets. He hoped Sierra wasn't the easily offended type; she didn't seem like it. Still, she seemed even less like the type to send him a bunch of tropical fruit and a bottle of cheap champagne.

"I don't think so," he said.

"You didn't? I was sure it'd be there when you finished the show. About five-two, blonde, pink and silver leopard-print underwear?"

"Excuse me?"

"Nice tight pussy, teacup tits, gag, and handcuffs?"

After ten years as a rock 'n' roll star, corrupting the morals of America's youth and driving the world inexorably toward Sodom, Spider just then discovered he could still blush.

"Looks like I got it after all," he said. "It was a lot better than a basket of pomegranates."

"Don't get me wrong," smiled Sierra. "She was just warming you up for me. And, for the record, I can live without the cappuccino."

"They've got decaf," said Spider.

"If I'm not mistaken, China'll have room service waiting."

Spider looked into Sierra's dark eyes for a moment, chuckled and took out a roll of dimes.

"Oh, please," said Sierra Verdi, breaking the roll open and fishing out a single dime. "No need to overpay."

The two of them left four dollars and ninety cents on the table—nice tip for an Evian. Luckily, Spider's cab was still parked outside.

DADDY'S GIRL

Marilyn Jaye Lewis

When my little sister, Jenna, and I were eight and ten years old respectively, we fell in love with an older girl, Denise Dominic, our babysitter. Denise lived three houses up the block from us and was one of seven black-haired children in an Italian Roman Catholic family. All the kids on our block went to public school except the Dominics—they attended Saint Christopher's and so seemed to inhabit a different planet.

Before Denise became our babysitter, when she was fifteen, Jenna and I knew nothing about the Dominic family except that Mr. Dominic had a wicked temper. His dark, Italian complexion grew even darker when he'd come out to his front lawn and holler for whichever one of his seven children had managed to fuck up at the time. The rest of us neighborhood kids would scatter for the safety of our own backyards when Mr. Dominic was on the warpath. Rumor had it, he beat his children with a belt when they were bad—a thing that didn't happen in the rest of our white, Anglo-Saxon houses, and so the unknown easily terrorized our immature but fertile imaginations.

Denise was a scrappy tomboy, even back then—and this is going back about eleven years already. It seemed like she was always in the doghouse for something. After Jenna and I had fallen in love with her, it was particularly gut wrenching to hear Mr. Dominic's booming baritone holler out, "Deh-*nise!* You get in here this minute!" Then that night, Jenna and I would hide together in the bed we shared and commiserate over poor Denise's fate; whispering in cautious terror, as if we were afraid Mr. Dominic himself would hear us from three houses away and, belt in hand, come after us next.

Denise became our babysitter when our regular sitter moved away. I was watching TV alone in the family room early one fateful Saturday evening, when my mom came in, followed by a tough-looking, black-haired teenaged girl with intense brown eyes. My mom said, "Jill, honey, you know Denise Dominic from up the block? She's going to be your new babysitter."

Well, technically, I did know Denise Dominic, but I'd never seen her up close before. I was instantly smitten. From that moment on, I had an acute attack of butterflies in my belly whenever Denise came anywhere near me. Jenna fell in love that very same night, but her infatuation with Denise didn't last as long as mine did, which is why what came later seemed so incongruous to me—but I'm rushing myself.

Jenna has always been more outgoing than I have. Even back then, she openly flirted with Denise—baited her endlessly or tried to amuse her—whereas I was painfully shy and easily intimidated. I often felt like Denise barely knew I existed since my sister took up so much of her attention whenever she was in our house. But luckily, Jenna went to bed a whole hour earlier than I did. That last remaining hour that I got to spend alone with Denise on Saturday nights was what I lived for through the week. Even though I rarely uttered a complete sentence to her, I pretended all week long that that coming Saturday would be the night I would finally confess my love to her. Of course it never happened.

The following year, my parents decided I was old enough to look after my little sister and myself. That was also the year Denise turned sixteen and wanted a better paying job anyway, so that she could buy her own car. My sister moved on to another infatuation—boys—while I stayed hopelessly in love with Denise from afar. By then it became difficult to catch a glimpse of her in person, she was so busy being a sixteen year old, but she filled my fantasies at night in ways that grew increasingly disturbing.

It used to be that Jenna and I confided in each other about our fantasies—especially the ones involving Denise. Remembering them now, I see that they were only vaguely sexual, but they led my sister and me to discover masturbation together, nonetheless. But as we grew older and Jenna's fantasies centered more around wanting to be touched by boys, I still lingered over visions of being touched by Denise, of spreading myself open for her, of having my mouth between her legs, and being overpowered by her. To the point where I fantasized that Denise was something like her father—that she would beat me with a belt, then expose and humiliate me and make me have orgasms in spite of myself. These were the disturbing fantasies that I couldn't bring myself to confide to anyone. Not even Jenna, who was usually lying right there beside me in the dark as the tormenting fantasies unfolded in my head.

One month before she was to graduate Saint Christopher's, something scandalous happened to Denise. I was only thirteen at the time and the significance of the vague rumor I'd heard went over my head, but it involved Denise and some other Catholic girl in the shower of the school's locker room, and Denise getting kicked out of school. I did know that Mr. Dominic beat Denise so badly for being expelled from school only one month before graduation, that she moved out of the house and took an apartment of her own on the other side of town. I didn't see Denise again for seven more years. And when I did see her, it couldn't have been under more jolting circumstances.

It was right after I dropped out of college and went back to stay temporarily with my parents. I already knew I was gay— there were no doubts left about that—but the suitable lover I sought was proving to be elusive. My first night home was a Friday and I decided to check out the sole dyke bar in town, the Jack of Hearts—an unassuming, unmarked, windowless dark hole off a side street in the heart of the old warehouse district.

It was literally only a matter of moments before I spotted her sitting at the bar. She was a lot older than the last time I'd seen her, but I knew it was Denise. I wanted her more than ever. She looked gorgeous, menacing, so grown up—everything I'd longed for in a female. Her black hair was chopped short. She looked lean and wiry in a black button-down shirt with the cuffs rolled up, a pair of blue jeans, and black combat boots on her feet. She was smoking a cigarette while she nursed a beer. My agenda fell together in my head quickly. First I would try to buy a drink without being carded, since I was still several months underage; next I would get up enough nerve to say hello to Denise.

I got past the first hurdle effortlessly. But just as I was getting up my nerve to walk over to where Denise was sitting alone at the bar, the incredibly femme girl who came out of the bathroom and then sat down beside Denise, slipping an arm through hers, turned out—to my horror—to be my little sister.

"Jill!" she practically squealed, noticing me right away. "What are *you* doing here?"

In as few words as possible, I managed to tell her I'd dropped out of school and had moved back home that very afternoon.

"You remember Den Dominic, don't you, Jill? Denny—you remember my sister, Jill, don't you?" Jenna looked at me as if she would burst with delight. "Denny and I are living together now," she gushed. "We have a cute little rental on the other side of the hill, off Main Street. You've *got* to come visit!"

I thought I was going to be sick. "Den" extended her hand to me. "Hey, Jill," she said. "Of course I remember you."

I shook her hand, looking into her dark eyes. "Hey," I choked. And I had nothing left to say after that. The electricity that shot through my bowels from simply shaking her hand made me so envious of my sister I couldn't speak. I left the Jack of Hearts shortly after that, halfheartedly promising that I would visit them sometime over the weekend.

Alone in my bed that night—the bed I had once shared with my little sister—my jealousy festered. It was clear our parents had no inkling either one of us was gay. I lay awake plotting childish revenge. I'd spill the beans at the breakfast table the following morning: "You two are so blind; can't you see that Jenna's gay?! She's living in sin with that dyke Denise Dominic!" But in my heart of hearts, I knew that if the tables were turned my sister would never stoop to betraying me. I managed to keep my mouth shut the following morning, and then swallow my pride and drive out to my sister's house that afternoon.

Now, in hindsight, I can't decide if that was the best thing I ever did, or the worst.

I found their little house easily and pulled my car into their driveway. The house seemed closed up, as if no one was home. Maybe they weren't awake yet? But I rang the bell anyway.

It was Den who opened the door. She was wide-awake. She

looked even more incredible than she'd looked the night before. She was wearing the same combat boots and blue jeans, but now she had on a tight, white muscle shirt, which showed off her well-developed arms. Her breasts were small and taut, her nipples hard and easily discernable through the thin cotton fabric. She wore a small silver ring in one ear and had an unassuming tattoo on her right forearm. A lit cigarette was jammed into the corner of her mouth. She opened the screen door slightly and stuck her head out. "Hey, Jill," she said, taking the cigarette out of her mouth and staring at me.

She didn't move aside, ask me to come in, or make me feel welcome in any way. I hadn't anticipated that so I just stood there stupidly and stared back at her. But what she said next was even more dismaying.

"Jenna's being punished. She's been bad. She can't really have visitors right now."

Her words were so unexpected; it seemed to take an eternity for them to even register.

"Your sister's a little tramp, you know that, Jill?" she finally continued as the cigarette went back into her mouth. "She made Daddy very angry today so she had to learn her lesson and then she got sent to her room. She's being punished—is there something about this you're not *grasping*, Jill? You have a weird look on your face."

I knew I had to be blushing crimson by then. I was so filled with embarrassment, envy, lust. The whole scenario seemed to be dawning on me in rapid progression: Den was "Daddy" and Jenna, the lucky bitch, was being taught a lesson—maybe even the hard way. I tried to pull my gaze away from Den's penetrating stare, but wound up focusing on her hard nipples instead. It instantly made matters worse in the envy and lust department and I knew that all of it was registering on my face.

"You wanna come in for a beer?" she asked suddenly, looking down at her watch. "Your sister's probably been punished long enough. I'll check on her in a minute and see if she's ready to behave."

I think I was secretly hoping Jenna would refuse to stop doing whatever it was she'd done so that I could get a little more time alone with Den. I followed Den into the kitchen and she handed me a beer. She stood blocking the doorway, making it impossible for me to stand anywhere in the tiny kitchen except uncomfortably close to her.

"Well, Jill, you certainly have grown since the last time I babysat you."

"Yes," I answered as casually as I could, secretly thanking god that she was still a little taller than I was. It helped nurture my meager fantasy. Even though I was still disbelieving that my sister was actually gay, I knew I could never make a play for anyone she was involved with, no matter how badly I wished I had it in me to do just that.

Den stubbed out her cigarette. "What were you doing in the Jack of Hearts last night anyway; looking for love or just a reasonable facsimile?"

"I don't know. Either one, I guess."

"So you've dropped out of school, huh?"

"Yes," I replied, taking a sip of beer.

"You're very pretty, you know that?"

She'd caught me off guard.

"What's the matter?" she asked. "Are you embarrassed to be so pretty?"

"No," I laughed lamely.

"I always knew you were going to grow up to be very pretty. Jenna's pretty, too, but in that over-the-top, super-femme way, you know? You—I can tell you wake up pretty. You just roll out of bed and look gorgeous, don't you?"

I felt like I was running a sudden fever.

She looked at her watch again. "Should we check on the brat now? I think she's been punished enough."

Not knowing what else to do, I followed Den to the stairway that led up to the small bedrooms. She stepped aside and said, "Beauty first," then followed a little too close behind me as I went upstairs. I could feel her eyes taking me in, checking me out.

At the top of the stairs, she passed me and said quietly in my face, "You have a great ass, you know that? I think it runs in your family." Then she put a finger to her lips and mouthed, "Shhh," while opening the bedroom door.

I wasn't expecting to see what I saw. I couldn't believe it was my sister.

"Hey brat, are you ready to behave?" Den asked as she entered the room. "A word of warning: we have company."

A blindfolded Jenna protested vainly through the ball that was wedged securely in her mouth and laced with a cord that was tied behind the back of her head. I didn't see the ball at first because Jenna was bent over a tall bar stool, her hair hanging down in her face. Her arms were outstretched; her wrists tied securely to two of the stool's legs and her ample tits looked uncomfortably heavy, hanging upside down from her birdlike rib cage. She had on a pair of painfully high heels with ankle straps that were attached to the other two legs of the stool. Other than the shoes, she was naked. She had a tattoo on her butt that I'd never seen before and her legs were spread just enough for me to see that her pussy was completely shaved. Something was stuck in her ass but from where I was standing, I couldn't tell what it was; I could only tell it was huge. And she had bright red stripes across her backside, clear down her skinny thighs.

"These are what started the whole brouhaha," Den announced, as her fingers retrieved a pair of pink lace panties that had been stuffed inside my sister's vagina.

Jenna groaned only slightly as the panties were pulled out, but when the huge plug was pulled out of her ass next, she grunted hoarsely as if she were in pain.

My heart was racing. I was torn between feeling sorry for my sister—wanting to bolt before she could find out it was me standing there and realize what I'd seen—and feeling utter contempt for her because I was still jealous as hell. If it had been anybody but Denise Dominic, I would have fled.

Den unstrapped my sister's shoes, releasing her ankles from the stool's legs, then untied her wrists. When she slipped the blindfold from Jenna's face, Den grabbed a handful of my sister's hair, lifted her up by it and said, "Look who's here."

It was then that I saw the ball in her mouth.

The blood had been rushing to her head for I didn't know how long, so it was hard to tell if she was actually embarrassed or not, but it was obvious that my sister was stunned to see me. She was unsteady on her feet when her body was finally righted all the way. She collapsed down on the bed and kicked off her shoes. She unwedged the ball from her mouth as she stared up warily at Den, who stood over her and said, "You want the panties now? Huh? How 'bout it, tough girl? You want to test me again?"

I had lived with my little sister long enough to know how she behaved when she'd been seriously punished, and the way she shamefacedly replied, "No," to all of Den's questions made me wonder just what the heck had been going on between them. Had it been some kind of a sex scene that they'd both gotten off on, or had Jenna just been incredibly abused?

Den picked up a pair of scissors that were lying on the

dresser, cut the lace panties in two and dropped them into a wastebasket.

On her way out the bedroom door, she winked at me, grabbed hold of my arm and said, "Are you ready for another beer?"

I didn't feel right leaving Jenna alone like that—especially since I wasn't sure what had happened. "Maybe I should stay with her," I said.

Den stopped at the top of the stairs and looked at me. "Why? She's okay. She's just gonna jump in the shower. She'll be down in a minute."

I felt more confused than ever.

Then Den seemed to notice the look of concern that must have been on my face. "Hey," she said. "What's going on with you? You don't think I'd ever hurt either one of you girls, do you? Come on, now. It's just sex. Let's get you another beer. I promise you, your sister's okay."

Like the proverbial yo-yo, I was jerked right back to feeling hot for Den again by the fact that she had even remotely included me in that statement. I followed her into the kitchen for my next beer, noticing that this time she also took a bottle for herself. Once again, she stood in front of the doorway, keeping me at an uncomfortable disadvantage. I couldn't kid myself anymore—I liked it.

"I'm sorry that whole scene upset you, Jill. I was just playing."

"I wasn't upset," I spluttered. "I guess, well, I just never expected to see my little sister like that. I never dreamed she was into that stuff."

"She's not, really," Den said matter-of-factly. "She's just trying it out. Experimenting, you know? She wanted to be my lover so I'm letting her be my lover—for as long as she can take it. But she's not exactly a natural, by any means."

"Oh," I replied a little hopefully, in lieu of saying what I was fully thinking.

"Hey," she said, moving a little closer toward me. "What are you doing this afternoon? Why don't you stick around? We have some friends coming over." Then to my complete amazement, her hand went under my shirt, expertly found my nipple, even though it was safely hidden inside my bra, and pinched it. "Don't worry about your sister," she said quietly. "It's not love, Jill. She's just killing time. You'll see."

I wanted to kiss her but nothing in her expression looked like she would allow it. She seemed content to pinch my nipple, tug on it through my bra and watch approvingly as my pelvis began to writhe. "You always were the one who behaved. Look at you. You never gave me any trouble."

By the time my sister came downstairs, Den and I were sitting like normal people on the couch in their living room. Even though I was in a veritable swoon and not really aware of anything but my hormones galloping through my body, I somehow managed to make what sounded to me like reasonable conversation. Because of my guilty conscience, it was hard to look my sister in the eye anymore, but I noticed that she seemed to be having just as much trouble looking directly at me, so I didn't feel quite so bad. And when their other friends arrived and the liquor began to flow, I saw with my own eyes what Den had said earlier about Jenna—she *was* a little tramp, planting herself in another woman's lap and making out with her in front of all of us.

It was then that I saw Den motion to me with her head to follow her upstairs. I couldn't believe my good fortune. I really couldn't believe it was happening to me. We weren't even halfway up the stairs—we were just barely out of sight—when Den pulled me up to the step above hers. "Take down your pants," she said.

"What?"

"You heard me. I said take down your pants. Come on, I wanna see your ass."

I did as she asked. With fumbling fingers, I quickly unzipped my jeans and lowered them down my thighs, tugging my panties down after them.

"Good girl," she whispered, grabbing me around my waist and pulling my naked ass up against her crotch. She reached down between my slippery labia, dipping into the wetness and sliding it all over my clitoris. I moaned. I couldn't help myself. Her teeth sank lightly into my shoulder. "You smell so good," she said quietly, sweeping aside my hair, her nose taking in my scent. "Kneel down for me, okay? Do it right now."

She let go of my waist and I knelt down on the stairs, tilting my ass up to her. She pushed my cheeks open wide and planted her mouth right on my asshole, her tongue coaxing the hole to relax and open for her. When it did, her finger slid up my ass and her mouth moved down to my swollen clit, sucking it in between her lips. It felt incredible—mostly because I couldn't believe it was Denise Dominic doing it. Finally.

She stood up abruptly and practically dragged me up the stairs. "Come on," she said, "let's get naked. Let's do this right." She pulled me into the bedroom with her and locked the door behind us.

I stripped out of my clothes and watched her strip out of hers. Her body was immaculate. Lean, muscular—perfect. But when she turned her back to me, I gasped. Her ass and upper thighs were covered in scars. "What *happened* to you?"

She shrugged as she strapped on a dildo. "The scars? A gift from my father, from when I got kicked out of school."

"Jesus," I cried under my breath.

"Yeah," was all she said, taking me by the arm and directing me toward the window.

I wasn't sure what she wanted then.

"Up against the glass. Come on, you know. Your tits; put them up against the window."

"But it's still light out," I replied incredulously. "People will see."

"Do it for Daddy, come on. I get off on it."

I watched her slather the fake dick up with lube. I got a funny feeling I knew where she was planning to put it. I wasn't sure I wanted to take that huge cock up my ass right in front of the window.

Den looked at me, rubbing even more lube onto the cock. "Come on, Jill," she said. "Do it for Daddy. Make me happy. I don't want to have to beg. It makes me angry to have to beg and then there's no telling what we're liable to get into."

I thought of my sister battened down over the bar stool, an even larger tool wedged into *her* ass. I went over to the window and did as she said, pressing my tits up against the cold glass. Den was right behind me, her slippery hands prying me open, pushing the head of the tool into my tight hole. It felt enormous. I wanted to cry out.

"Don't," she encouraged me. "You're a big girl now, you can take it. I know you can. It hurts a little, I know, but soon you'll be begging me to fuck you like a dog, you know it."

I did know it. I tried to relax and take it all the way up without flinching. In a matter of moments she was fucking me savagely, stuffing my ass. It felt so good. I was oblivious to being in front of the window, my tits pressed flat against it, in full view of anyone who might happen to walk down the street. "Oh yeah," I was ranting, "fuck me."

After a few minutes, she pulled me away from the window and tossed me onto the bed. "Come on," she said. "Beg me. Beg me to fuck you like a dog."

"Fuck me like a dog," I begged, assuming all fours as she mounted me, the dildo pushing into me again, filling my ass, stretching me open all the way.

"Louder than that. Beg like you mean it."

"Fuck me like a dog," I cried, as she pumped into me hard. "Fuck me like a dog!"

"That's right, Jill. Who's your Daddy?" she asked, slapping my ass.

"You're my Daddy."

"I can't hear you," she said, slapping me again, her hips increasing their rhythm almost viciously—I had to hold on to the bed.

"*You're* my Daddy," I cried desperately. "Fuck me like a dog, Daddy."

"That's good. That's right. That's what I like to hear." She plowed her full weight into me, toppling me over, but we stayed coupled; my asshole impaled. She lay on top of me, catching her breath, her breasts flat against my back. She smoothed my hair away from the side of my face and her mouth found my ear. "Who's your Daddy?"

"You are," I panted. I couldn't remember ever feeling so completely aroused.

"You want your ass to belong to Daddy? You want your pussy to belong to Daddy?"

"Yes," I whispered. "Yes, I want that."

"Show me how bad you want it, Jill. What are you going to do for Daddy?" She eased the dildo out of my ass, lifted her weight off me and waited.

I didn't have a clue what she might have wanted me to do. I acted on impulse. I turned over, faced her, pulled her down onto me and kissed her mouth ravenously, wrapping my arms and legs around her tight, getting her as close to me as I could.

She kissed me back for several seemingly eternal moments. When we came up for air, I couldn't help myself. "I love you, Denise," I said.

It was clear she wasn't accustomed to being called Denise anymore. I was afraid I might have spoiled the moment.

"I know you love me," she said. "Your sister told me."

I suddenly felt like an idiot. "She *told* you? When?"

"A while back; when she and I first started going out. Hey," she said. "Come on, relax. We're here now and it's working, right? Let's just see where it takes us."

But where could it possibly take us as long as she was still living with my sister?

"Just let Jenna play out," she said. "Girls like her always move on. She can't handle me and she knows it. What about you? You think you can handle me?"

"Yes," I answered, not entirely truthfully.

"You sure about that, Jill? I'm a mean motherfucker when I want to be. I'm a tough Daddy; I learned from a pro. He was the meanest motherfucker on the block."

"I know," I said, looking up into her face and catching a glimpse of a different kind of darkness, hiding at the edges of her eyes. Part of Mr. Dominic was in there somewhere. The full impact of it made my heart race: she was actually dangerous.

"If you behave, Daddy's going to be good to you, Jill. But if you play with me, I'll mess you up. You're saying you can handle that?"

"Yes," I said, hoping I sounded convincing; wondering how well I would fare on the day she decided to snap.

"Then we're good to go," she said, getting off me, her feet finding the floor. Then she grabbed a handful of my hair. Guiding me off the bed, she said, "On your knees, honey. Be good to Daddy, now."

I positioned myself between her legs and tried to reposition the dildo so that I could get at her clit.

"No, no, no," she corrected me, putting the dildo back in place and pressing the head of it against my lips. "Do it the way the Dominics do it; be a good girl for Daddy."

I took the huge fake cock into my mouth and let her find her own rhythm with it—working it in and out. I held on to her legs as her fist held tight to my hair and a chill ran through me. "That's right," she chanted. "That's right, honey. Be good to Daddy and Daddy is going to eat you up. Daddy is going to give it to you the way his little girl likes it. Just as long as you behave."

And even though I was writhing over every exquisite minute of surrendering to Denise Dominic at last, I had a sick feeling down in my belly that her own daddy, the formidable Mr. Dominic—the meanest motherfucker on the block—was even meaner than he'd looked and probably should have been shot. "Do it the way the Dominics do it," Denise had said, forcing me to suck her cock as she had probably learned long ago. "Be a good girl for Daddy."

THE DISCOVERY

Rachel Kramer Bussel

It wasn't until a year into our marriage that I discovered it. Up until then, I thought Brian was a normal guy. Not boring, but not the kind with any secrets stashed away, because I'd know about them, right? But then one day I was sorting through our things in the attic and found a carton filled with all manner of porn—box after box of dirty videos, each more salacious than the last, with girls tied up, their mouths open, their breasts bulging forward; and magazines where girls bent over and got spanked by muscular men wearing little more than tight underwear. As I pawed through the box, unearthing images I'd never even come close to imagining, what surprised me the most wasn't that Brian, *my* Brian, owned and obviously valued these items enough to take them with him and keep them hidden, but how hot they were making me. It started slowly, but by the time I pulled out the last video, which featured two girls tied up together, their bodies spread into positions of total submission, clearly about to have countless wicked tortures unleashed upon them, I had started to want to see more, had started to imagine myself in their position, had started to get wet at the prospect. Why hadn't Brian ever told me about this?

As if in a trance, I put everything back in the box, but took one video back downstairs with me; noting that I still had an hour left before Brian would get home, I slipped it into the VCR. Well, if the covers had gotten me turned on before, watching the actual video was something entirely new. From the minute the first scene unfolded, featuring a young, busty woman rolling over in bed, offering up her legs and arms to be secured to the bedposts with rope while her boyfriend's cock bobbed up and down, I was a goner. I didn't touch myself, didn't have to yet, but my pussy was absolutely throbbing, so wet that I feared I might soak the couch cushions. I was so entranced as I watched that first girl get fucked while she writhed against the ropes—even with the sound muted I could hear her screams of delicious agony—that I didn't quite hear Brian's car pull up or him walk in the door. So that's how he found me—sitting in front of the TV screen, mouth hanging open, legs spread, utterly engrossed.

"Hey, baby," he started to say before he looked at me, then the TV, then back at me, as his mouth formed a similar O of surprise. I slowly reached for the clicker and turned the video off. The silence rang through the room, and I could feel my heart pounding within my chest, partly with arousal, partly fear. Now we were even, perhaps—I'd caught him with his little hiding place, but he'd caught me enjoying his private stash. I knew he didn't know what to make of his discovery because he just stood where he was, his mind clearly spinning as he tried to process this information.

"I...," I stammered, then took a deep breath. "I was cleaning the attic and found this box with your videos, and I was curious and put this one in...," I said, my voice trailing off, not sure how to continue.

"And?" he prompted, his eyes searching mine as he took a tentative step forward.

"Well, I've been looking at it and...I want to be mad at you, but I can't...because I'm too turned on. I want to be like the women in these pictures, I want you to tie me up—" I couldn't even continue because just picturing myself splayed across our bed, while Brian secured my wrists to the bedposts before ravaging me in the most ungentlemanly way possible, had my whole body lit up with desire. I could feel goose bumps forming all along my arms; my nipples beading up and my pussy churning, tightening so fiercely I thought I might orgasm right then and there. I was sure my face was bright red, but Brian was my husband—surely he'd understand.

"Really, Nance? Are you sure? I'm sorry I hid them from you all this time. I was just sure that you'd be upset or offended, or just wouldn't understand. I never in a million years would have thought you'd want to do that," he said, indicating with a nod of his chin the video box covered with naughty images, "with me," he finished.

We both stared, surveying each other in the light of this new information, before moving into the bedroom. We'd always had good sex, fun sex, pleasant sex but, truth be told, never the kind that I could honestly say had made the earth move. I'd usually come, sure, but never with the screaming, wild intensity I'd seen in the video, never with the kind of power that made me feel like my head might literally explode. But already, as Brian reached forward and took each of my wrists in his strong, large hands, I could feel myself inching toward that rocket ship of pleasure that I hoped would soon send me soaring into a new universe of arousal. He massaged my pulse points with his thumbs, pinning my arms down to the bed as he hovered over me. That action alone made me catch my breath. I was ready; in fact, I was more than ready, I was primed and eager for him to turn me into his bound beauty.

"Yes," I whispered, though my straining arms and spread legs surely conveyed what I wanted. He kept me pinned there with his arms and his eyes, his gaze searing into me, and I didn't need to look down at his crotch (though I did, briefly) to know my submission had made him hard with desire. He let go for a moment, as if to see what I would do, and I stayed in place, my arms above my head, my body bared just for him. I swallowed, my throat suddenly tight as I waited for him. *How had I gone my whole life without ever succumbing to this most exquisite state?* I wondered, as he took a coil of black rope from the back of a dresser drawer. I didn't stop to think where he'd gotten it or how long he'd had it, or whether he'd ever planned to share it with me. He took off my clothes and then wrapped the rope loop by loop around my wrists, keeping them strained above my head where I couldn't see. I gasped as I felt the rope, softer than I'd have expected, pressing against my tender wrists. He jammed a finger between the rope and my skin as he tightened the loops around me, and when he slipped his finger out and made the final knot, tugging on it to make sure it was secure, I moaned. I felt like I'd landed in some other world, playing the part of some porn vixen, yet I was also fully in the moment, alert and aroused. I knew that if I could have slipped my hand down to my cunt and stroked myself just once, I'd have found my sex shockingly wet. Brian's chest hovered above me as he kissed my bound palms, nipped at each one with his teeth before moving on to suckle my fingers. I stretched out my tongue, wanting to taste his salty skin, and finally he lowered himself so I could lick along the hairy surface of his chest. He slowly slithered along

my body until his weight was pressing down against the length
of mine.

I could feel his cock pressing against me through his jeans,
and with my feet planted firmly against the bed, I lifted my hips
up to meet his, grinding against him while he leaned down and
kissed me. His tongue pressed powerfully against mine, and I
breathed in quick, erratic spurts while he took a leisurely tour of
my mouth, edging along my tongue, then up against my teeth,
then my gums, then tracing my lips. I shut my eyes as he kissed
my face slowly, tenderly, each brush of his full, closed lips
against my skin taking me higher and higher. He kissed his way
downward, traveling along my chest, briefly licking my nipples
until they were wet and erect and straining for more, then kept
going, tickling my stomach before reaching my cunt. His breath
and tongue were hot against my flesh as he toyed with my clit,
granting me only the briefest of strokes before he stopped. "I
forgot something, honey," he said, and I couldn't imagine what
it could be as my pussy convulsed, missing his touch.

Then I felt him wrapping more rope around my left ankle,
preparing to fasten it to the bedpost. I looked up at him, not
sure what I wanted. I bent my elbows slightly, moved my arms
as much as I could, and experienced a corresponding tug deep
inside me. I quivered as he secured my other leg, leaving me
literally wide open for him. "You look so beautiful like that,"
he said softly. "I can see everything," he continued as he slowly
took off his clothes. I watched as he unzipped his jeans, then
pushed them, along with his underwear, down over his cock,
which sprang forward. I'd been looking at his dick for years but
somehow this time it looked bigger, thicker as he stood there.
My breathing got heavier and I whimpered, bucking against
the rope as I tried to reach toward him. "I know, sweetheart,
I know," he said, even though I hadn't spoken. He stood at

the end of the bed and stroked his cock, gracefully sliding his fist along his shaft, teasing me. Normally I love to watch him pleasure himself, and have even spied on him for brief moments when he didn't know I was watching, but being unable to move and so horny I thought I would scream, was driving me mad. Finally, Brian took pity on me, or perhaps was just overcome with his own urgent arousal, because he pounced. First, he slid two fingers fast and deep into my pussy, not giving me any warning. I clamped around him, the sensation compounded by the delicious tension traveling through my arms and legs, which seemed to reverberate back and explode in my pussy. When he pulled his fingers out, they were glistening with my juices, and he sucked on them, smacking his lips.

Finally, after what felt like an eternity, it was time for me to receive his cock. Usually I'm an equal partner in our sex sessions, but this time, my only task was to lie there and take him into me. Being so passive was a sexy change, and I waited, not that patiently, licking my lips and holding my breath until Brian saw fit to plunge his cock inside me. As he pushed his way inside me, I rocked against the bed, the backs of my hands brushing against the headboard. I moaned as I struggled, my movements making his cock slam harder against me, giving me just the rhythm I desired. Every move his dick made inside me seemed heightened, and I struggled for breath, for sanity, as he slowly moved in and out, savoring his power over me. My legs were trembling, and he placed a hand on my thigh, pinching that tender, sensitive flesh as he thrust inside me. His gaze met mine; my eyes felt luminous with arousal and love as I offered myself to him. Not just my pussy, not just my spread legs and bound arms, but *me,* all of me, every last bit of my body and soul, and he took it, gratefully, gracefully. Brian leaned down, gathering me in his arms, smothering me with kisses as his cock speared me over and over again, claiming me, as I sobbed tears of joy and surrender into his neck. When my climax overtook me, it felt like I'd been blasted from a cannon, sent up into the sky to twirl and twirl, tumbling over myself, then somehow falling back down to earth with the safety of a parachute. His arms cradled me, and he softly, slowly, pumped his last few thrusts into me as he came.

When we were both done, he quietly untied me, stroking my slightly reddened wrists and ankles, both of us still entranced by what had just happened. I had gone from total innocent to bondage queen in one fell swoop. I pulled Brian close to me, grateful that I had a man whom I could trust with anything and everything and that now, finally, he could do the same with me.

COWBOY'S DUNGEON

Michelle Houston

Hanging her Stetson carefully on the hat-hook just inside the barn door, Natalie stepped into her husband's playroom. Over the years, he had slowly added more and more sexual toys, until the room could rival any city man's dungeon of depravity. She paused just inside the threshold and inhaled deeply, savoring the scent of tanned leather and sweat. If she listened closely, she could almost hear the echoes of her moans and screams from the night before.

Trembling as memory nurtured the embers of her lingering passion, Natalie made her way further into the room. Ahead of her, along the back wall, stood a giant wooden cross to which her husband often strapped her by her wrists and ankles, and whipped her ass to a rosy hue. Whips, paddles, and chains adorned one wall, while along the other, a row of mirrors gave a hint of class to the sawdust-covered floor.

As she reached the center of the room, Natalie paused again. She ran her hands over the waist-high, saddled "horse," and felt her jeans growing damp.

Attached to the ceiling, the contraption was a long wooden bench that hung a few feet from the floor. What held it in place were the ropes run through a series of pulleys and levers, which, at the flick of a switch, would rock Andrew's invention back and forth. The saddle was a traditional western saddle; the stirrups were the perfect length to help Natalie remain balanced.

A quick glance at her watch made Natalie gasp: it was almost 3:00 p.m., and Andrew had ordered her to be mounted and ready for him. Hurriedly, Natalie moved to the row of mirrors and stripped. Neatly folding her clothes, she laid them on the bench in the corner.

Crossing the room, she pulled a harness and dildo from a shelf, as well as a tube of lubricant. She coated the dildo with the clear gel before she thrust it into her pussy an inch at a time. By the time the toy was in to the hilt, her body was covered in a fine sheen of sweat. She wanted to lie down on the floor and fuck herself to an orgasm, but she knew Andrew would know if she did, and she wasn't about to do anything to upset her master.

After a quick wiggle of her hips to make sure the dildo was firmly in place, Natalie stepped into the harness, and pulled it up her waist, setting it in place. She made quick work of the series of buckles and straps, familiarity making her task easy.

Once she had the fake cock in place inside her body, Natalie stepped back up to the horse and mounted. With minutes to spare, Natalie had time to reflect on the toy that was buried within her clenching pussy.

Firm, and curved at the tip, it was her favorite dildo. With every breath she took, the head pressed and rubbed against her sensitive walls. She couldn't help but moan softly and shift, manipulating the cock against her G-spot.

Minutes passed, as the leather saddle beneath her ass grew

slick from her sweat and her essence. Gripping the pommel, Natalie squirmed and wiggled, trying to find relief, which she knew wasn't available to her. The dildo nestled deep within her was designed to make her aware of every nerve ending in her pussy. It was intended to increase her sexual frustration, to heighten her pleasure—and Andrew's. It would only be with the swinging motions of the horse, operated by Andrew, that she would achieve orgasm.

Gazing at herself in the wall of mirrors was another form of sensual torture that Andrew demanded. She could see her nipples standing out hard and proud from her chest, tiny silver rings dangling from the tips; her skin glistened. The ropes holding the horse in place creaked as Natalie shifted again.

A faint breeze stirred the air as Andrew opened the barn door, announcing his presence.

"Been waiting long?" he drawled.

"No, Sir. I was mounted and ready at three." Keeping her gaze focused on her reflection in the mirror, Natalie fought the urge to squirm again.

The long curved vibrator pressed directly on her G-spot, and she craved to succumb to the gushing orgasm it could bring with the right help.

She could hear Andrew's steps behind her as he crossed the room, settled into his chair, and began to work the ropes. Natalie knew it wouldn't be long now.

The horse bucked back and forth, grinding the pommel, which she was gripping tightly, against the base of the harness. Digging her heels firmly in the stirrups, she tightened her thigh muscles and held on for the ride.

The smooth leather beneath her ass rubbed her inner thighs and buttcheeks as she shifted slightly backward. On the back swing, she shifted forward.

Faster and faster the horse rocked, until Natalie couldn't control her reactions anymore. Moaning and arching against the pommel, she drove the cock as far into her quivering pussy as the harness allowed and climaxed deliciously.

The motions of Andrew's invention slowed, until it only swayed slightly.

"Did you like that?"

"Yes, Sir," Natalie whispered, her breath coming in gasps.

"Dismount." The slow drawl of his voice was gone, replaced by a clipped forcefulness. Andrew was a country boy at heart, but he was also a very dominant man.

Legs shaking, Natalie slid from the horse and stood waiting. Bracing herself with a hand on the damp leather, she turned to face her husband. His damp, curly hair; clean jeans and flannel shirt made it obvious he had stopped for a shower after tending to the fence in the east pasture. He had pulled on his clean boots, which lacked the mud and manure that clung to his work boots.

"Come over here, and bring a paddle with you." Mind racing, Natalie tried to think of what she had done to deserve punishment.

Walking across the room as fast as her legs would carry her, Natalie quickly selected his favorite paddle and presented herself to Andrew. Dropping to her knees, she lay her head on his inner thigh and waited, the paddle clutched in her hands.

He smelled of sandalwood soap and leather, of sex and cologne.

Inhaling deeply, Natalie resisted her desire to nuzzle her nose in his jean-clad crotch. She loved to bury her face in the tiny curls of hair around the base of his cock after he had showered.

"Climb up here," he demanded, patting his thighs. Her legs less shaky, Natalie stood at Andrew's side. After handing him the paddle, she bent over at the waist, and let him guide her into position over his thighs.

"Now I want you to know something, Natalie. I love you, but you deserve a paddling. You left the door open on the chicken pen, and we lost several good hens. So be a good girl, take your punishment, and we can move on to the real reason we're out here."

The paddle smacked against her damp flesh.

Yelping softly, she relaxed her body, eager for the next swat. Again the paddle smacked her tingling flesh.

She knew she had made a mistake, and deserved punishment. While she enjoyed the paddle's sting, she knew that every time she sat down over the next day she would be reminded to double-check the pens.

Another smack, harder than the last. Natalie winced slightly at the sting, even as her pussy clenched around the dildo.

Again and again Andrew rained blows on her tender ass, until they were landing in a continuous blur of euphoric sensations. Each instinctive jerk of her body twitched the harness, shifting the cock that was still strapped within her.

Lost in the slow buildup of her second orgasm, Natalie at first didn't notice the paddle had stopped falling.

"I think that's enough for now. You should be nice and tender for a while."

Natalie wanted to wail "No," to demand that he swat her a few more times.

Her pussy was already spasming around the dildo. Just a few more swats would send her over the edge again.

But she knew better than to beg for more. This was Andrew's domain, and in here, she did as she was told. She also knew any more swats might make a gentle reminder a painful one.

"Stand up."

Legs shaking, Natalie complied. Andrew smoothly stood, his toned body rippling with the motion, his flannel shirt pulled tight against his corded muscles. Natalie felt her legs weaken as always, watching his movements.

"Remove your harness, darlin', and bend over and grab the arms of the chair."

The smooth drawl she loved so much was back, melting her a little more inside. When she had first met Andrew, his smooth voice had nearly made her cream her pants. Nothing had changed in the five years since.

With shaking hands, she worked to remove the harness. She was always surprised that it took longer to strip off the harness than it took to buckle it into place. As the dildo slid free from her weeping pussy lips, Natalie shuddered and almost melted into a puddle on the sawdust-covered floor. Her clit throbbed, aching for contact.

Resisting the urge to finger herself to another orgasm, Natalie bent over and gripped the arms of Andrew's chair so tightly her knuckles turned white.

"Relax." Andrew stroked a finger gently up and down her spine. His calloused hands smoothed over her tense muscles and relaxed her.

Slipping his fingers down to her asscheeks, he gently parted the globes and slipped a fingertip into her crack. He teased around her sensitive nether hole, making her scream internally for penetration. As if he heard her thoughts, he pressed a finger on her hungry orifice, slipping past the fluttering muscles. Pushing firmly, he worked his finger and slid it all the way in, stretching her tight rosebud.

"Relax," he drawled again. Natalie's head fell forward and she turned slightly, so she could see almost everything Andrew was doing in the mirrors.

She felt empty when he removed his finger from her anus. She watched in the mirror as he bent forward and picked up a tube of lubricant from the floor.

Popping the top, he pressed the tip against her puckered hole and squeezed.

The cool liquid trickled into her hole and coated her crack. Recapping the tube, he tossed it aside, reached behind his back, and pulled something from his back pocket. "I've got a little surprise for you," he said. Natalie almost whimpered as she saw the size of the odd-looking butt plug he held in his hand, with the tuft of long horsehair attached to the base.

Pressing it firmly against her ass-bud, Andrew twisted the plug as her muscles stretched and gave way, the flared base lodging tightly against her anus.

"On your hands and knees."

Natalie tried to gracefully drop to the ground, but the sensation of the large plug nestled in her ass caused her to twitch and shudder along the way. As she settled herself, she felt the tail brush against the back of her legs and she knew what Andrew wanted. He had recently shown her some pony-play erotica on the Internet.

Trying to mimic the sounds of their horses, she tossed her head back and neighed.

"Good girl." Andrew's praise encouraged her to work harder to imitate what she had never before tried. Shifting her hips, Natalie tried to prance slightly, without being told. Around his chair she circled, showing off her sleek lines.

After her fourth turn, Andrew reached out a restraining hand. Gripping her hair tightly, he pulled her head back. "Shhhh, girl. It's okay, baby. Stand still."

Natalie trembled as his hands stroked down her spine, along her side and around to the mound of her mons.

"Such a nice filly you are. Someone has been taking very good care of you, haven't they?"

Andrew stood and moved around behind her. He held her still with just a finger thrust into her creamy heat. Natalie could hear the sound of his jeans being unzipped behind her. Pretending nervousness, she shifted from side to side, neighing softly and nodding her head back.

"Shhh, girl. Shhhh. No one's going to hurt you. Just relax. That's a good girl." Andrew kept up a steady stream of soft-spoken words as he moved her tail to the side, pressed his cock against her pussy lips, and thrust.

"Oh yeah, such a good filly."

Natalie clenched her pussy tight as Andrew withdrew and thrust in again, deeply. His hands gripped her hips, holding her still for his assault.

She wanted to beg him to go harder, to fuck her senseless, but she also didn't want to lose her role in their game.

By neighing louder, she hoped to convey her demands. Tossing her hair, she arched her back and gripped his cock tighter.

One of Andrew's hands left her hips and tangled in her hair, pulling her head back farther. "You like that, little filly?"

Natalie neighed as she pushed back into the curve of his groin.

"You like being ridden rough?" he asked softly, his fingers digging tighter into her hip. Leaning down, Andrew bit the side of her neck as he slammed into her pussy, taking her with an animalistic passion.

Natalie knew she would sport some bruises in the morning, but didn't care.

Her body screamed for more, she was lost within a maelstrom of passion.

Her voice hoarse from neighing so much, she whispered

Andrew's name softly, her body convulsing in orgasm.

Her body quivering, she felt Andrew pounding into her pussy, until with one last thrust he collapsed against her back, pushing them both to the sawdust-covered floor.

Natalie struggled to regain her breath as her body hummed. Feeling completely drained and lethargic, she couldn't summon the energy to roll over when Andrew flopped onto his side next to her.

His hand slid down her back to her ass, where he grabbed the base and gently removed the plug.

"I love you, baby," he drawled, his voice husky. Tenderly, he placed soft kisses along her back and still rosy asscheeks.

"I love you too, Master."

"As much as I would love to lie here all night kissing and caressing you, I think we are in need of a shower." Andrew stood and helped Natalie up, then swept her into his arms.

"Thank you," she whispered. She nestled her head in the crook of his neck as he carried her out the barn door. "I love you too, Andrew."

"My pleasure darlin'. You did good, very good. And that's good, because there are some more things I want to try out, real soon."

SONNET

Cate Robertson

When a master craves the body of his slave more than the air
he breathes, who is the master and who is the slave?

Idly contemplating this conundrum, he sat before the late
news with a knob of ginger and a paring knife, a cloth spread
on his lap to catch the thin parings. His brow puckered with
concentration as he scraped and carved the firm creamy meat of
the root into a cylinder about an inch thick and three inches long
with a rounded tip and a substantial flange at the base.

Watching the news was a ruse for Emma's benefit.

"Are you coming to bed yet?" she had asked.

"No, I'll be up when the news is over."

He twirled the finished pillar of ginger between his thumb
and forefinger, examining it in the blue glow of the television for any bumps or protrusions. He gave a satisfied grunt.
The shape was perfect. The cool moist flesh oozed a faint but
sharply scented dew that could temporarily scald the most
intimate mucous membranes of the human body with a heat

that might make a man lose his mind or renounce his God.

He shuddered with delight, picturing the effect on her.

"Animated" was how the websites described the victim of figging. For twenty minutes, the ginger plug would fling her into a paroxysm of agony. Then it would be all over, with no harm done.

The perfect torture. For the perfect woman.

Sonnet, his dark-haired and milky-skinned slave. But who was slave and who was master, when he craved her flesh like a drug? When just the thought of her full breasts with their thick rosy nipples and her soft, silky arse threw him into raptures? Fashionistas would condemn her as plump but he thanked god for her luscious cheeks and thighs. There was so much more of her to savor than you'd find in those scrawny coat hangers of girls his colleagues trotted out as mistresses.

Sonnet. My darling Sonnet.

Just hearing her name in his mind's ear made him rigid.

Before going up to bed, he diced the ginger into the kitchen compost and dropped the paring knife into his briefcase in the breakfast nook. He had the technique down pat now. He would sculpt the next one before her eyes.

As he lathered and scraped his face in the morning, he was still thinking about her, but when was he not? He could see her on the bed, so helpless, so beautiful.

How odd, that such a chance encounter can change a life. That a young woman could plunge a man deep into his own unconscious sludge and bring him face-to-face with the fearsomely twisted demons that lurked there. Where were such creatures spawned? And how is it that she brought them out? Was he destined to confront them, if there was such a thing as destiny?

If there was, Sonnet was his.

In the café, after months of dalliance online, she had made no bones about her intentions. She was a slave seeking a master: a man who would own her sexually. Whenever he wanted her, she would be there for his pleasure. Whatever he wanted to do with a woman, he could do it to her. She needed—*needed*, she emphasized—a man to whom she could refuse nothing.

How long had he borne with the refusal of almost everything in his own marriage bed? On impulse, he said, "I'd like to try to be that man for you."

And he was, two months later, clattering down the stairs and whistling like a schoolboy.

"You're chipper this morning," said Emma as she buttered the toast.

"Well, it's Friday! Oh sweetheart, that reminds me. I meant to tell you. I'm staying over in town again tonight. I'm sorry." He crunched his toast nonchalantly, scanning the business section.

"It's okay, darling. I'll go visit Mother. How are those meetings going, by the way?"

Oh, the perks of heading up the corporate section at the firm: she never complained about his overtime, and he could book the suite at the Carlton on his personal expense tab. These meetings with private clients—*all rather hush-hush, you know*, he'd wink—always detained him so late he might as well stay overnight.

He shrugged. "It's hard to tell. You just have to schmooze them for a while and see what happens. I take it one meeting at a time."

He didn't know her real name. She was writing her thesis on some arcane aspect of Elizabethan literature, so when she asked him to give her a slave name, it seemed apropos. He'd always loved Shakespeare, and here she was, a dark lady of his very own.

His first gift after naming her was a small but hefty hand-stitched octavo edition of the sonnets bound in red morocco, tooled and gilded. She appreciated its considerable value. She turned immediately to her favorite, LVII, and recited it to him:

> *Being your slave, what should I do but tend*
> *Upon the hours and times of your desire?*
> *I have no precious time at all to spend,*
> *Nor services to do, till you require...*

As her first task of obedience, he required her to have a tattoo inscribed in her furrow behind. He showed her where. *LVII* in a small, elegant Latinate font.

"To remind you who is your master," he told her, but in fact, it would remind him whenever he caught sight of it.

The train journey to work was a pleasure on the days he chose at random, once every other week or so, to arrange for her to be there after dinner, waiting for him in the suite. When the time came, she would take his coat and briefcase and answer his questions, then ask for his instructions.

"Where do you want me, Sir...? How may I please you to-night?"

The hypnotic clackety-clack of the wheels, the sleepy jostling of other passengers induced him to lean back with half-closed eyes and conjure her up. Where he wanted her and how. In which delicious pink orifice, because he loved them all. How he would control her: bind and curb her cruelly, then whip her on-ward, forcing her through orgasm after orgasm, using her until he was sated and she was exhausted.

It was more than her body. It was the eager and whole-hearted way she deferred, surrendered, obeyed. The piteous way she begged for his mercy, the valiant way she endured his voracious assaults on her. The way she gave him everything: her pleasure, her pain, every last shred of her dignity.

How she whored and abased herself for him.

It made him ravenous for her.

At lunchtime, he went out to shop. Despite the generous payments—thank god, money was no obstacle for him—he always brought her a little gift, something precious like a gold choker or a jeweled silk thong, or something playful like a pair of ben wa balls. He loved the way she would lay her elegant hands like two slim white birds against her throat while she cooed over his gifts.

But today his destination was rather less romantic than the jeweler's or the sex-toy shop. Today he stopped at the greengrocer's.

He searched the displays for just the right fist of ginger. He found an imposing specimen with a vaguely threatening aura thanks to its rude and bulky digits. Thick, firm, and fearsome, he felt certain it was something she would never forget. The clerk dropped the thing into a paper sack.

As soon as the office closed and the secretaries had left for the day, he called her. He had given her a phone for his calls only, with instructions never to turn it off and never to call him.

"Are you ready for tonight, darling?"

"Yes, Sir. I can't wait to see you, Sir."

He closed his eyes. Her voice at once was a balm to his soul and a fiery prod to his desire. "Good. Be nice and pretty for me."

It wasn't necessary to remind her. She'd helped write their rules. She would be flushed clean and scrubbed pink from clit to rosebud, plucked and waxed with a light fragrance at the throat only. Scented soaps and body lotions were forbidden because he wanted the female flavor of her skin, the unsullied tang of her sweat, the rich bouquet of her animal juices.

He took his time over dinner in the hotel dining room, knowing that she was upstairs, waiting for him, dressed in something shockingly indecent, growing damp in her fidgety eagerness to please him. So close, so deliciously close now. In the men's room, he flossed, brushed his teeth, and loosened his tie for a casual air.

He straightened his shoulders and ruffled his fingers through his thick gray hair.

> *...what should I do but tend*
> *Upon the hours and times of your desire?*

Oh dear god. How could she be more beautiful each time they met? The patent stilettos tensed her calves and thighs while the fore-and-aft dip of the saucy black corset drew blatant attention to her divide, and as for that creamy strip of skin above the lace edge of her hose: his mouth watered.

She kissed him, took his jacket and briefcase and placed the paper sack on the bedside table without a murmur, then turned and stood demurely for his inspection. The corset exposed her cunt and cupped her breasts underneath to show her naked nipples. Her pink parts must be always accessible. That was the rule. On the rare occasions he took her out in public, she was permitted neither bra nor panties.

He walked all around her. At a word, she bent forward to let him examine her cheeks. He kissed them, but he felt like tearing into them with his teeth.

"You've only got one little red mark left from last week, darling."

"Yes, Sir, thank you."

"I'm glad. I never want to leave any permanent marks on you." He examined her nipples, setting a tender kiss on the rosy and protuberant tip of each one. Ever since the night he had bound her and made her come from nipple twisting alone, he had made a special study of nipple torture.

"Fetch the weighted clamps."

Her breath caught, but she obeyed, fetching them from her case. They were the most vicious pair he possessed and the ones she feared most, with rubber-coated steel jaws and ovoid silver weights. As he tightened them, she chewed anxiously on her lower lip.

"Have you been training your nipples as I told you?"

"Yes, Sir, every day."

"Bring me the pictures."

She fetched them, swaying and bouncing, and wincing with each bounce, giving him yet another chance to say *Alleluia!* for the inventor of six-inch stilettos. The pictures were perfect. As instructed, she had slipped tight little elastic O-rings over the base of each nipple to make it swell and redden. Twenty minutes, three times a day.

"What do you think about when you wear these?"

"I think about you, Sir. About how much I want to please you."

"Do they make you horny?"

"Oh yes, Sir. Very much so. Horny for you, Sir." She smiled seductively. "Do you want me in the shower now, Sir?"

He smiled down at her. Little vixen. "Not tonight, darling. Just get ready."

He shaved again, then lathered and luxuriated in the steam, giving her time to prepare, allowing his own desire for her to suffuse his veins like wine.

When he emerged, everything was ready. On the low dresser,

she had laid out the paddles and floggers that he had entrusted to her care, along with his collection of vibrators, gags, dildos, and nipple clamps. On the bedside table she had placed the crystal decanter of single malt, with two fingers poured and waiting for him.

She was kneeling on her elbows on the four-poster, wearing her dog collar and heavy-duty cuffs at her wrists and ankles. She smiled at him over her shoulder and waggled her arse. Fucking little whore. The lips of her cunt showed like a puffy pink pistachio between her thighs. He suspected she had been playing with herself. He took off his robe and moved around the bed, his silk boxers well-tented. What huge erections she gave him, thick and steely. It was like being twenty again.

"Give me your hands. Lean forward. I want to rig you higher today."

He secured her wrists to a point well up the bedposts, so that her arms stretched out at shoulder height. Her whole upper body from the hips would be suspended from her wrists. How prettily the weights hung down! He gave them a twirl, just to hear her grunt in pain.

He buckled her ankles to the three-foot stretcher bar and strapped that firmly to the posts, pulling her knees back until her whole upper body was suspended from her wrists. She was poised, like an eagle about to swoop.

His nostrils flared as he inhaled the heady female perfume of her spread cunt. He was delighted to notice the trail of ooze high on her inner thighs. "You little slut. Look how wet you are."

"I know, Sir," she whispered.

"Were you playing with yourself before I came in?"

She nodded in shame.

"You know the rules about that. You must be punished for playing without permission."

She nodded. "Yes, Sir," she whispered.

"Would you like your bunny?"

"Yes, please, Sir." He inserted her favorite pink rabbit and set the remote on random. Then he retrieved the paring knife from his briefcase and sat in the chair beside the bed, sipping the whiskey and watching her. "I suppose you're wondering what I've brought you today." Nonchalantly, he opened the paper bag and withdrew the monstrous root.

Her brow furrowed in a question, and then her eyes widened as she realized what he was planning.

"You know what this is." She nodded and swallowed.

"Do you know what I'm going to do with it?"

He was taking his time, selecting just the right digit, finally deciding on the longest, thickest one, a plump hard digit about four inches long and as thick as his erect cock. He took out his knife and sliced it off carefully. Then he began to peel it as he had done a dozen times before, his practiced fingers moving deftly over the crisp creamy flesh, dropping the papery skin in little shards, sculpting from an ugly root a shapely and massive plug with a wide shoulder that tapered for a bit before it flared out to the flange.

"This will hurt a bit, my darling."

Her eyes glistened, brimming with tears. "Yes, Sir. I know."

"But you deserve it. You've been a very naughty girl, haven't you?"

"Yes, Sir."

She jumped and moaned as the rabbit pulsed suddenly, then whimpered as the weights bobbed and swayed in response. He half-closed his eyes, near ecstatic with lust. The poor baby! Her pain had to be excruciating. Her nipple flesh was an angry red, and as taut as stretched elastic in the terrier-like jaws of the clamps.

And now to teach her real agony.

He stood up, smiling, and twirled the plug close to her pretty face, already red and wet with tears. "Take a good look. Do you think this will do, sweetheart?"

She made a little animal sob, whispering, "Please, Sir. Please don't put that…"

Dear god, how could a woman be so beautiful in her helplessness? Already her shoulders gleamed with a sheen of sweat and her hair stuck to her forehead.

Soon enough she would be streaming and soaking that lovely basque with her labors. As for her cunt, the bunny was doing its relentless work, pulsing sporadically inside and outside, and the steady trickle down her thighs was all the proof he needed that she was teetering on the brink.

"Don't put it where, sweetheart?"

Her voice was barely audible. "Please. Don't put it up my arse, sir."

He chuckled. "Oh, but I must, baby. You need this lodged deep into your arse, and for a long time. Tell me why."

She choked back tears. "Because I need to be punished, Sir."

"And what else?" He gave a tug on the weights. It was a signal for her to give the correct response.

"Because I need. To be reminded. Who owns me, Sir."

"And that would be…?" Another tug, much harder. She threw back her head and gasped.

"You. You, Sir. You own me."

"That's right, my darling. What a clever girl you are!"

He was almost afraid he would unload right there, spontaneously, into his boxers, or into her face. He moved behind her and spread her delicately, exposing the lovely private tattoo that marked as his exclusive territory the sweet flesh he had purchased and maintained as a private playground.

She was breathing raggedly, with little rhythmic pleading whines that maddened his blood. Her furrow was so mocha-pink and clean, he couldn't resist pushing his face into it, rubbing his nose and chin into this sweet forbidden dampness while his cock throbbed with the anticipation of possession. He kissed and licked with gusto until she sagged against the restraints, groaning in ecstasy.

"Tell me what you are."

"I'm a filthy whore," she moaned.

"My filthy whore," he corrected her, growling. "This is to make sure you never forget it."

With her rosebud slick with spit, it just needed a gentle circular prodding, then one nice stiff push, and the thick digit sank deep, right to the shoulder of the flange. One more shove, and her sphincter gripped the narrow neck with a visual, if not audible, *pop!* that made her shriek.

What followed, he remembered in a haze of pre-orgasmic bliss. She didn't scream so much as howl. Her voice soared into registers he had never heard from any human throat and raised the hairs right down his spine to the core of his own arse. She roared as never before, not even during the most severe canings, which had left red stripes a half-inch thick across her snowy cheeks. Fearing the management, he hastily strapped on her ball gag but even then, he had to grab her hair in his fist to keep her head still.

As for her exertions, he weighed the chances of either the bed or her joints flying apart under the strain of her adrenaline-fueled panic. Her dance of agony beautifully exemplified that old conundrum of physics: irresistible force meeting immovable object. She would heave herself forward in a desperate attempt to escape the pain burning up her behind, only to intensify it when her cheeks tightened inadvertently on the plug. The pain reflex drove her backward onto her bent knees, but then the bob and jolt of the nipple clamps made her lurch forward again. All the while, the bunny's pulsations made her hips gyrate in a desperate attempt to come through all the pain. It was hypnotic, like watching a complicated mechanical device, and a noisy one at that.

But of course she was flesh and blood pushed to the limit of endurance, and all the while she writhed and bucked, her face streamed with tears and her eyes begged him to release her.

After fifteen minutes, he could wait no more. It was time to mount her and collect her, time to drive her onward. He knelt behind her and removed her bunny, leaving the ginger simmering in place. He sank by degrees into her as she involuntarily fucked herself backward onto him. He leaned forward, tugged off the gag and clamps, and knotted his fingers into her hair.

She came, and came, and came again, clenching on him and screaming something that he couldn't hear because he was busy with his own labors, climbing, scrambling, and clawing his way up to the summit. With a shout he sprinted, flinging himself up the slick slope of her flesh while she tightened her grip and yanked him onward, calling—he could hear it now—his name, crying and laughing and singing it. When he flew out into space, he felt a roar erupt from his own throat, but only when he was falling through space did he realize he was moaning, shouting, calling a word. Her name.

Sonnet. Sonnet. Oh my darling Sonnet.

Munching his room service toast point, he poured a coffee and took it to the bed. She turned tousle-haired from the pillow, her face wan and sleepy.

"Coffee, darling?"

Her breasts jostled as she pushed herself up to a sitting position. Her nipples were raw and still impressively large, he noted with pleasure—they were responding nicely to his program of continuous rough stimulation—but he didn't touch them. He could have. He could hurt her, but to what end right now? In the rights he had purchased of her, he practiced mindful cruelty, not mindless malice.

"Thank you, Sir." She took the mug with a grateful smile and drank. Then she touched herself with a fingertip and hissed. "Oh my god, Sir. I'm so sore."

"You'll heal in a few days, my beauty. I won't give you nipple exercises this week."

"Thank you, Sir. But I hope I may serve you some other way?"

He smiled. How aptly, yet how naturally, she phrased herself. Not, *What do you want me to do,* but *Please may I do something for you?* "Let's continue the theme. I want you to masturbate every day with the pink glass dildo behind and the bunny in front. Send me pictures from your webcam."

"Oh, yes, Sir. Thank you. That will be my pleasure. Sir, I have to say something about last night. When I came, Sir, did you notice? I said your name. Without permission. I'm sorry."

"Sonnet, you never need permission to say my name when you come. In fact, I think you should have to."

She threw her arms around his neck and kissed him with an impulsive display of affection that wasn't covered in the rules. "Yes, but Sir, I just want you to know that I said your name, not because I had to. Because I couldn't help it."

Damn her. Yes, he bought her services, he paid her well— handsomely, in fact. Yes, according to their rules, he owned her. But who was to say who was master and who was slave? Because as surely as he buckled her to the bed and made her scream, just as surely had she enthralled and shackled him; and just as he had sounded the depths of her pain, so had she guided him, far beyond the boundaries of rules, to the unknown cloud-capped peaks of his own pleasure.

He spread her tenderly right there and had her again, with his tongue deep in her mouth forcing her to hum with delight. He couldn't help it any more than she could.

ORDINARY
LOVE

R. Gay

I enjoy tormenting my wife, Sasha, because she lets me. Sasha lets me torment her because she enjoys it. We play little games, share mutual fetishes. She likes watching me chop onions before I fuck her over the kitchen counter so that she can taste their bite and cry without cause. I like watching her humiliate herself for me. There is a balance between us. "Andrew," she'll say, while we're sitting next to each other on the train, on the way to work. There's always urgency in her voice and I know what she's going to say before the words fall from her mouth. I'll turn to look at her, then look away, quietly observing the other passengers—the way the man across from the aisle from us adjusts himself when he thinks no one is looking, the way the woman in the row in front of us keeps jerking her head, trying to stay awake.

While I'm watching all this, I'll turn toward her, slide my hand across my left thigh to Sasha's right, squeezing gently, slipping my fingers beneath the hem of her skirt. She'll clear her throat and look out the opposite window at the passing scenery, a light pink blush spreading across her face. She'll pretend to be somewhat disturbed. But she'll brush her thumb across my wrist, and lean closer into me. We'll stare at each other in these moments, and the rest of the world recedes. All I see is my wife, her legs spreading ever wider as we pass New Rochelle.

Later, always, I smell her on my wedding ring.

Sasha enjoys these torments because she appreciates the view from the bottom. She told me this on our third date. She was kneeling on the floor of my apartment, smiling up at me on the couch, my pants around my ankles. "I don't care what you think of me," she said, with a little laugh. "I like the view from down here." And with that, she swallowed the length of my cock, continuing to laugh. I could feel the vibrations of her throat muscles. It was a curious sensation.

Sasha carries her secrets in tight knots along her spine. When she's lying in bed, her back facing me, I can see their outlines in the dark. Sometimes, I reach for her to trace them with my fingertips. She shrinks away, curling herself tightly. I withdraw but continue to watch. Sometimes, after we've shared a bottle of wine and we're on the couch watching television, she'll dance around her secrets, try to share a part of herself, but she never gets too far. I don't push. I don't want to complicate the games we play with history.

We married after dating for only seven months. I proposed to her after a free jazz concert in Central Park. We were sitting on a bench, where she was trembling and smoking a cigarette. It was cold and windy and miserable. I put my coat around her shoulders, knowing it would smell like tobacco for weeks afterward. It was not a moment. I didn't make promises I couldn't keep. But after I asked and showed her the ring, she took a long drag on her cigarette and answered, "I'm going to say yes because I think you have the capacity to hurt me the way I need you to."

People think they know Sasha. When they see her, they think she is a slender, cheerful young woman who is always in a good mood. I see Sasha, with her arms bound behind her back so tightly that her elbows are touching. There is anger in her eyes and her lips are swollen. She is seated on a wooden chair, her breasts thrust forward, a thin silver chain between her nipples. I am standing, one foot on the chair between her thighs, only a few inches away from her cunt. She looks right through me as she tries to inch forward, create a point of contact between us. I simply smile.

Sasha wants me to take her somewhere—a place she has no vocabulary for—a place neither of us have been. I can hear it in her cries when we're fucking, or I'm stretching her limbs across our bed or we're crammed into the antiseptic space of the train bathroom. I can always tell that we're not quite there yet. It creates tension between us. Tonight, I wait for Sasha to return home from work. She is late, as usual. I never know where she goes after work. I don't ask. I am in our back yard listening to the night when I feel her cool hands on my shoulders. Without turning around, I say, "You're late."

"I know," she replies and returns to the house.

I finger my belt buckle, and stand, slowly. I find Sasha in our bathroom, undressing. She smiles at my reflection in the mirror, unraveling her hair from the two platinum hair sticks she uses to sweep it up most days. When she sets them on the counter, the sound echoes through the room. She quietly slips out of her dress and I glance at the scars along her upper back—scars for which she offers no explanation. Lower, there are scars that I have given her.

The thin, slightly braided scar just above the crack of her ass, that runs the width of her back, I gave to her in Miami. We were staying in one of those boutique hotels in South Beach. We came back to our room after a night of strolling Collins Avenue, drinking mojitos, dancing to *la musica Cubana,* pretending we were people different from ourselves. She quickly undressed, splashed some water on her face and crawled into bed with my straight razor. She crossed one leg over the other, the tip of the open razor pressed into her knee. "I once saw this movie," she said, trailing her hand along the empty space next to her.

I knelt at her feet, pressing my lips against the exposed soft spot of her inner ankle. I slid my hands up her muscled calf, slightly gritty with sand. She uncrossed her legs. I lay atop her, letting her feel the full weight of my body. Sasha's chest tightened, her breathing grew increasingly labored. I kissed her, roughly, sliding my tongue into her mouth, across her teeth. I freed the razor from her grip, set it on the pillow next to her face. My hands, still rough with sand, slid between our bodies, up her torso, around the outer curves of her breasts. She arched upward and I moved my lips to her neck, tugging at the taut skin with my teeth until she gasped, loudly.

I turned Sasha onto her stomach and lay next to her, one of my legs draped over hers, my mouth at her ear, whispering to her about all the things I would do to her that night and every night thereafter. I called her the names she likes to be called— whore, slut, mine. I took the razor and slid the dull edge along her spine and across her back, navigating the tightly knotted secrets and scars. I stopped just above her ass, pressed the sharp edge of the razor at one end of her back and quickly drew it across. She hissed as tiny droplets of blood appeared. I tossed the razor aside, and inched her thighs further apart. We had seen the same movie. I raised her ass toward me and slid my cock inside her. It seemed like all the muscles in her body tensed. She reached back without ceremony, digging her nails into my skin, urging me deeper. Afterward, I told her I loved her, the way I always did. I touched the drying blood. She sat up, wrapped the sheet around herself and lit a cigarette. I watched the silhouette of smoke curl around her. Sasha, a longtime Johnny Cash fan, smiled at me and whispered, "Love is a burning thing."

I want to know the stories of all her scars, but I'm not sure I'm willing to pay the price for that knowledge. Sasha continues to stare at my reflection. She is an expert at holding a gaze. She won't break—not for anything. She's that way about many things. She turns around and leans back against the bathroom counter. I pull my belt free from my waist and wrap it around her throat. She arches an eyebrow, feigns boredom. Sasha is very good at pushing buttons.

I cast my eyes downward and she reaches forward, unzips my slacks, slides a hand into my boxers. Her touch is cold and I shiver as she begins sliding her hand up and down along the length of my cock. She is neither gentle nor rough. My jaw clenches and I clear my throat. I don't want to give her the satisfaction of knowing how much I enjoy her touch. When Sasha brushes her lips across the tip of my cock, before wrapping them around, flicking her tongue against the wet slit, I stop her, push her away. It is a rough, unkind gesture. Still holding the end of my belt, I start walking away. When there's a tug, she starts to crawl after me, tentatively at first, then faster to keep up.

When I stop at the foot of our bed and turn to look at her, she is less smug than she was before. "You have not come close," she says.

"To what?"

"You'll know when you get there." She sits cross-legged, waiting for my next move. We are, I think, very large chess pieces. I cup her chin with my hand, pulling her mouth open. She tilts her head back, her hands holding my ass as I begin to slide my cock in and out of her mouth with slow, deliberate thrusts.

Every now and again, she closes her mouth slightly, letting her teeth graze against my shaft. I slide my fingers through her dark hair, closing them into tight fists. Sasha brings one of her hands to my balls and grabs them between her fingers, grasping as tightly as I have a hold of her. I grunt, try to twist away, but her grip is steady and unforgiving. I thrust harder, faster. She makes muffled coughing sounds. After I come, I stagger. Sasha wipes her lips with one thumb. She swallows. She waits for my next move. I'm not sure, but I think I hear her say *Check*.

Sasha hates having her pussy licked. Nothing gets her angrier than when I tie her down and lie between her thighs, lavishing my tongue across her swollen pussy lips and hard nub of a clit. She won't speak to me for days afterward. When pressed, she says that it bores her and lacks purpose. But she comes when I put my mouth on her and it's the only time she makes any real sounds—high-pitched moans that she utters at a staccato pace. I pull her onto the bed, and slide my hands up her inner thighs. The muscles flex. I press my forehead against the mound of her pussy, breathing heavily. She smacks my forehead, but I push her arms away, sliding my tongue inside her cunt before drawing it up toward her clit. Sasha digs her heels into my back, just beneath my shoulder blades, far harder than necessary. When I look up, I see her head turned to the side, tears of anger threatening to spill over the crests of her eyelids.

"Do I have you where you want me to have you?"

"Fuck you," Sasha says. It is a wonder she can get words out through teeth clenched so tightly. I thrust two fingers inside of her, deep and hard. She winces. I slide my fingers out, then drag them up her body, between her breasts, leaving a damp trail. I straddle her waist, squeezing her breasts together. There will be bruises here. I reach over to the night table, and fumble for a pair of handcuffs. Defiantly, Sasha throws her arms above her

head. I clasp the cuffs around each wrist. Sasha shrugs. I slide off
the bed and tell her I'll be back. I wait in the hallway just outside
our bedroom. I can hear frustration in her breathing. She mut-
ters unkind things about me.

I go to the den and turn on the television, loud, letting her
hear it. Twenty minutes later, I hear footsteps. "Now, we have
a problem," I say. She stands in the doorway, her hands cuffed
in front of her. She looks lonely, abandoned. She is beautiful. I
stand and quickly close the distance between us. Clasping her
throat with one hand, I force her against the wall. I smack her
face, once, then reach down between her legs where she is wet.
I turn her around and kick her legs apart. One of her cheeks is
pressed against the wall, her eyes are tightly shut. I rub my hand
across her ass, pulling my fingers along the cleft before smacking that ass once, twice. She makes no sound. I smack her again,
hard enough that the palm of my hand tingles. She stands on
the tips of her toes, offering herself to me. I spank her until my
arm is heavy and the muscles in my shoulder burn. We are both
sweating. She is raw. Strands of her hair are plastered against her
face. When I scratch her reddened ass, it leaves white streaks.

This time, when I slide my cock inside her pussy, she moans,
loudly. "That's fucking right," I tell her. I call her my bitch and
tell her I want to hear just how much she wants this. She raises
her arms over her had, her cuffed fists resting against the wall.
To every question I ask, she gives me the answer I want to hear. I
twist her nipples with the fingers of one hand, and stroke her clit
in tight, fast circles with the fingers of the other. Her head rocks
from side to side. I want to overwhelm her with stimulation.
We are loud and vulgar. Our damp bodies come together and
fall apart with sharp sucking sounds. She is liquid heat around
me and I want to reach into the marrow of her with my lips, my
fingers, my cock. In moments like these, her rough edges fade.

Her arrogance retreats. Her body feels incredibly small and fragile. She is truly mine. I sink my teeth into her left shoulder, biting through the sweaty skin, then circling my tongue over the indentations. I kiss the back of her neck, and slow the rhythm of my hips.

Suddenly, I want to be gentle with her. As if she can sense what I'm thinking, Sasha says, "Don't," her voice hoarse, almost trapped. The tension in her body begins to slacken. When she comes, I can feel her pussy pulsing around my cock. Her body heaves with sobs and slowly, she falls to the floor. I look down at her, stroking my cock. She is clearly tired, but she knows what to do. Her face shines, her lips are slightly parted. This is my way of marking her, staining her with my seed in silver streaks across her face. And when I am spent, I am the one leaning against the wall. She lies at my feet, bent and slightly broken, her arms wrapped around my legs. I touch the top of her head. Before long, I will help her up, carry her to bed. We share an ordinary love.

UNLIKE THE
OTHERS

Xavier Acton

You've been a very naughty boy," Paige told him. "And you know what you deserve."

She knew him only as "Mike," though it was almost certainly not his real name, judging from the hesitant way he had pronounced it when he first introduced himself. She didn't particularly care what his real name was, though she preferred clients who weren't hiding anything. Still, Paige was a newcomer to the world of professional domination, and times were tough; she needed all the work she could get.

Besides, he knew Paige only as "Mistress Dominetta," the somewhat ridiculous name the proprietress of the Fantasy House had assigned her when taking her on as a professional dominant.

And, in any event, Paige was having some trouble concentrating on anything about Mike except the way he looked standing naked before her. The other three clients she had seen so far had all been more than twice her age and not especially interesting;

Mike couldn't have been older than twenty-five. He was buffed and toned as if he worked with a personal trainer and he had a series of tattoos up and down his arms. Up till now, Paige had not found herself the least bit turned on during a session. Not by the golden shower client who wanted to call her "Judith," not by the flogging bottom who took dozens of heavy blows without flinching or responding—a "black hole bottom," another employee of the Fantasy House had warned her. And certainly not by the guy who wanted to sit in a chair across the room and masturbate while she read aloud from *Down Under Lover*, a tattered porno paperback from the '70s.

This time, though, Paige was already uncomfortably turned on. She supposed she should work it to her advantage, but she only found herself blushing as she looked at Mike's cock, erect, angled rakishly and pointing at a phantom spot directly above her head.

Mike was totally unlike the others. He was cute enough for her to probably have asked out, stupidly, awkwardly, if she'd met him in another context. He was polite, respectful, and, Paige suspected from the way he had obediently undressed when she'd snapped her fingers, deeply submissive.

Mike wanted a spanking. An over-the-knee spanking. When Paige had talked herself into becoming a professional dominant, it had mostly been because she figured she could give men spankings and enjoy it, since the idea turned her on and she'd read plenty of spanking porn. Now, Mike would be her first paid spanking.

"Yes, Mistress," said Mike, his voice meek. "I've been very naughty. I know what I deserve."

Summoning her most dominant sneer—though she was still working on it—Paige snapped her fingers and pointed at her lap.

"Yes, Mistress," said Mike, and dropped to his knees.

"Did I give you permission to crawl?" she asked, stealing a line from the pro domme she had observed on her first day.

"No, Mistress," said Mike, and got to his feet. He walked over to the chair where Paige sat, and crawled over her lap. The Fantasy House had built the perfect spanking fixture for five-foot-three dominants like Paige to spank six-foot-plus submissives like Mike: it was a big padded chair without arms, but with a slightly raised padded bench on each side. Mike fit neatly into it; his knees sank into the padding and his arms hung over the side of the left bench. His cock pressed against Paige's thigh through her rubber dress. The feeling gave her an unexpected thrill, and she shifted uncomfortably under him.

Paige realized nervously that Mike had positioned himself with his ass on her right.

"You've done this before," said Paige.

"Yes, Mistress," said Mike.

"But you forgot to ask Mistress if she's left handed."

Mike's eyes widened; he had the look of a scolded puppy.

"Are you?"

"Would I mention it if I wasn't?"

It kind of scared Paige how good she was at being a bitch. Mike got up off of her, leaving a glistening sparkle where his cockhead had touched her dress. With her other clients so far, the sight of their come had been more than a little freaky for her. This time, she felt a little rush of excitement.

Mike obediently placed himself over her lap again in the opposite direction, the weight of his body lessened by the benches. His ass was tipped up at a perfect angle; he had only the downiest dusting of hair on it. Paige let her hand rest on his ass.

"You're very hard," she said. "If I spank you, you're going to come all over my dress."

"Only if you give me permission, Mistress," said Mike.

Paige felt her nipples harden.

She brought her left hand down on his ass firmly, heavy on the palm, the satisfying slap sending a pulse through her body. Mike twitched and then pushed his ass higher in the air.

"Naughty boy," she said, her own heat rising as she spanked him. "Very, very naughty boy."

"Yes, Mistress.

"Did I give you permission to agree with me?"

"No, Mistress."

Paige spanked him harder, picking up speed; his flesh reddened as she rained blows upon his muscled ass. She was more than a little bothered by how much the feel of it turned her on. That made her spank him harder, which didn't help the situation at all.

Neither did the bouncing of Mike's cock against her as, holding his ass up for her to spank, he jerked and writhed with each blow. The slap of his cock on her thigh was heavy, and when a little droplet of pre-come missed the hem of her short dress and landed about halfway up her bare thigh, she was shocked at herself for liking it.

"Thank you, Mistress," said Mike.

Irritated by how turned on she was getting, Paige growled, "Did I give you permission to thank me?" and began spanking him more rapidly, alternating from one cheek to the other, feeling his muscles harden and flex under her hand as the sting of the spanking mounted. His "No, Mistress," was lost in a whimper of pain, a whimper that sounded pathetic in a young man as buffed-looking and hot as Mike, which only made Paige's blood surge more. Breathing hard, she took a break to stroke her hand all over Mike's ass. He moaned as she teased the reddened skin, squeezing it with her fingers, pinching it. Mike's splayed legs revealed his balls, and the cock jutting down her thigh. She had anticipated this moment. She knew as a domme she would be expected to give hand jobs sometimes, but she'd always kind of dreaded it. She had rehearsed her professional hand jobs with a mathematical precision, imagining that if she performed her duties just so, she wouldn't have to touch the cock in question too much.

Impulsively, she reached between Mike's legs and grasped his cock, and not because he'd asked for it—he hadn't. In fact, it was an odd sensation for her to realize that she was stroking Mike's cock simply because *she* wanted him to come.

Her fingers closed around the shaft and she stroked all the way to the head. She felt the slick wetness of his pre-come on her hand, and began to jerk him off in earnest.

Mike moaned and pushed his ass higher into the air.

"You're a very naughty boy," said Paige, lost in the way his hard cock felt in her hand as she stroked it. "Very, very naughty. Very, very, very—"

"I'm going to come, Mistress," said Mike. "May I have permission to come, please, Mistress?"

"Not yet," said Paige breathlessly, fighting down her impulse, surprised that she didn't want it to end yet. She released his cock reluctantly and quickly returned to spanking Mike, harder this time; as aroused as he was, he could take more sensation. With each slap of his cock against her thigh, Paige fought the urge to seize his cock and stroke him till he came. Instead, she spanked him faster and faster until her palm hurt and her left arm felt like rubber. Then, hungrily, she grabbed his cock again.

"Mistress—" he began.

"Fucking come already," Paige said, her voice hoarse, the words springing unbidden to her lips, and she hadn't even finished saying it before Mike let out a thunderous groan and she felt the warmth on her thigh through the leather dress. Another spurt followed that one, and several more in rapid succession. She supposed that was why the chair was covered in vinyl.

"Thank you, Mistress," said Mike, and Paige withdrew her hand. She was a little surprised at what she did next; seizing Mike's hair in her right hand, she brought her left hand, sticky with come, to Mike's face. She had always thought she would wear a glove, but she'd forgotten.

And the sight of Mike obediently licking her fingers clean sent an unexpected thrill through her.

"I'm sorry about your dress, Mistress," said Mike when she withdrew her hand. "I'll pay for the cleaning."

The dress was rubber; Paige planned to wipe it down, but she wasn't going to argue.

"Yes, you will," she told Mike.

"May I do something for you?" asked Mike, his face turned toward her but his eyes still downcast; his full lips parted, tongue glistening with his own come.

Paige felt her clit throbbing under the soiled dress, her nipples so hard they tented the rubber. She felt a powerful urge to push Mike to his knees and shove his face between her thighs. But that would have been out of the question.

"Not today," she said. "Come back again, and we'll see. You're dismissed."

"Yes, Mistress."

Mike got off of Paige's lap. Paige tried very hard not to squirm in the chair as she watched him dress. She was still turned on, her pussy and clit and nipples uncomfortably engorged with blood. Mike methodically put on his jeans, polo shirt, and black oxfords. Before leaving, he paused, then walked back over to her.

"May I kneel to thank you?" he asked.

Paige's eyes narrowed and she pressed her thighs together.

"No funny stuff."

"No, Mistress," he said.

"Then, yes."

Mike knelt in front of Paige with his eyes lowered and said, "Thank you, Mistress." She hadn't noticed him palming the hundred-dollar bill; he placed it on the bench next to her and said, "Thank you, Mistress, again."

Paige had to fight the urge to giggle at the sight of the tip.

She nodded at him coldly. "You are dismissed until next time."

Mike got up and walked out without looking back.

"Jesus fucking Christ," said Paige, taking a deep breath. She got up and took a wad of paper towels from the dispenser on the wall. She wiped off her dress—good as new, almost—and tossed Mike's wad into the small garbage can in the corner. She could feel her thighs quaking, her pussy was hot and sticky under the rubber dress. She could feel the sweat pooling in the small of her back and the hum of arousal that made her want to get off right then and there. She resisted the urge only with a Herculean effort.

She picked up her hundred-dollar tip and headed for the dressing room. She was *definitely* going to take a cab home.

THE REAL PRIZE

Mia Underwood

I knew right away that I'd be good at the game. Holding myself totally still for long periods of time is something that I do well. I never need cuffs, don't require ties. I think blindfolds are for novices. My ex-boyfriend used to pride himself on how well I obeyed his commands. Since our breakup, I'd been lost. Without Justin, there was no order in my life. No need to behave, to be a good girl and do what he said. To be a bad girl and press the limits until he had to take me down a notch or two. Until he had to mete out the sort of punishment that always works to make me calm.

"Bad girl," he'd hiss. "Bend over and hold onto your ankles. Don't stand up, now. Don't you disobey me, Stella—" And then his fingers would slowly—so slowly—slip my silky panties down my thighs, capturing me in an embrace of lace. The feeling of being exposed would make me tremble, and I would have to fight within myself to stay still. I couldn't let him down so quickly. Yes, I'm a talented submissive, but it's a struggle every single time.

Justin understood that inner turmoil. He wouldn't start right away. He'd make me wait until my muscles trembled and ached. Until I was on the verge of standing up and turning around. That's when the first blow would land, restoring my faith both in his power as a dominant and in my ability to surrender.

Justin usually started simply, delivering a basic spanking using only his strong hand on my bare ass. Warming me with his palm on my naked skin. His hand was large and firm, and he could cup one of my asscheeks in his palm and squeeze, leaving a medley of memory marks for me to admire later. Only after he'd heated me inside and out would we move on to the next step in the passion play. His belt. His buckle. The bone-handled crop waiting patiently in the stand by our bed. He'd raise the stakes every time—how much of myself was I able to give him?—and I'd push ever onward to please him.

After he left, chaos reigned, and for me there was emptiness in the anarchy. So when I read about the contest in the paper, my immediate thought was: *Rules. I can follow rules.* My next thought was this: *That car is mine.* Keep my hand on a part of the sweetly polished chassis for hours? Christ, I could do that in my sleep. Let's see the rest of the naive contestants hold an arched-back position over a smooth wooden horse, praying silently for the burning kiss of the whip. Glistening drops of sweat beading up and sliding down. Tears imminent but still somewhere off in the distance. Waiting, without flinching, for the pain to begin.

Besides, what did I have to lose? For once, the only person for me to fail was myself. Yet for three days before the contest began, I was awash with jitters. Nervous excitement pulsed through my body. The only way I could relieve my growing tension was to come. Sex—even solo sex—has always equaled relief to me. Sprawled on the bed, legs apart, hands busy between my slender thighs, I thought about discipline, the discipline of complete submission. I remembered Justin telling me to behave for him, commanding me to show him what I had in me.

"That's right, Stella," he'd say, his fingers probing the slicked-up split of my pussy lips. "You deserve this. Just look at how wet you get when I spank that haughty ass of yours. Don't even try to deny it," he'd tell me, a dark pulse of humor in his voice. "Your body doesn't lie."

Over and over, I made myself come to old memories. Sticky and wet, I'd fall into sex-sodden sleep, imagining that I was holding onto a car. Imagining that someone was fucking me up against the back bumper. Justin, lifting me up, spreading me out. Just like in that old Pretenders song. "He's got his chest on my back across a new Cadillac...."

Was it healthy to live in the past? Probably not. But ultimately I didn't have the strength not to. Fingers probing, pushing deeper, clit sore from constant contact, I'd revel in the taste of metal in my mouth that always heralds an orgasm for me. Leaning back on the cool mattress, I would think about Justin reaching for the crop. I would remember rolling over for him, gripping the white down pillow and offering myself up. In my head, I saw myself absorbing the first blow, wetness of anticipation already leaking down my thighs; saw myself raising up for the second strike, then the third, slipping one hand under my body to stroke my clit and hearing him say, "Baby, did I say you could touch yourself?"

Until finally it was time.

The dealership was about a mile from my house, where the more quaintly residential area of Melrose and Fairfax gives way to the ugly paved flatlands of Pico Boulevard. I walked, to give my body time to stretch, strolled past the worn-down exterior of the New Beverly Cinema, was cruised by the tourists thronging to the French Market. I knew that if I really wanted to win, I'd have to go in for the long haul. Mind over body. That's always the most difficult part. Weak mental thoughts will sabotage even the strongest contenders. I've seen that happen often enough at the clubs I frequent. It's not the pain that makes you cave. It's the *thought* of the pain. How much will it hurt? How much will you be able to take?

At the dealership, a mixed crew of contenders had already gathered, each one hoping to drive away with the bright red automobile. They jostled around in the glassed-in enclosure, kidding each other into thinking that they had a chance.

That car's mine, I thought again after sizing up the competition. There were housewives and jocks, down-and-out businessmen and overly aggressive teenagers. But nobody looked the slightest bit tough. *No problem at all,* I thought, and then my gaze found him, a man who wandered through the automatic glass doors as if he had come to claim his vehicle. He didn't seem to see the rest of us, eyes only on the prize. But my eyes were fixed on him. Mesmerized.

Dark features, sleek hair, tall lean body. There were tattoos glazing his pale skin under that black long-sleeved T-shirt; I could see them in my mind. Maybe a piercing or two. Maybe more serious scars than that. He looked like the kind of guy who acted first and thought about the repercussions afterward. Finally, he locked eyes with me and then he half-smiled and gave me a nod. I understood his body language instantly.

You and me, he was saying. *These vanilla creatures all around us are no problem at all. It's you and me. Bet on it, baby.*

I tilted my head and gazed back at him. Smack in the middle of straight society, we were obviously two of a kind. I looked down at my well-worn black jeans, dyed and redyed so many times that even the creases were inked. I had scuffed black Docs beneath, a formfitting silky shirt of midnight blue. My hair was raven's wing black this week, and my silver gray eyes were outlined with a smudge of deep gray kohl. Hollywood rock 'n' roll meets gothic princess. That's my everyday attire.

Had I seen him before, or was he just one of the many in the sort of crowd that I run with? The type to go to the vampiric after-hours parties. Sleep in until noon. Live in a storefront on Sunset where he would possibly work the tattoo pen himself. Or even strum some fantastic guitar worth more than anything else in his apartment. I could picture it all easily. Hot plate in the back. Marlboros by the carton. So what was he doing here, at daybreak, in the middle of the asphalt jungle? That was easy enough—he was here to win a car.

The dealership owner brought my mind back around to the present with a quick pep talk. The rules were simple. Keep one hand on the automobile at all times except for designated breaks: a five-minute quickie every two hours. One ten-minute breather every four. Last man or woman with a hand on the prize would get to drive away with the car. "When we held the contest last year," the owner said, "we were here for almost two-and-a-half days. So I hope you people have a lot of stamina," he hesitated, and then added with an annoying guffaw, "and big bladders."

That having been said, we all found our spots and started... stopping. That's really what it was like. Stop your thoughts. Stop your mind. Stop your body from needing to move. Go deep inside yourself, into a cocoon. Hibernate. At least, that was my game plan. It's the same way I act when I'm on the receiving end of a whip. Hold still at your very core and quiet the inner screams.

Other people nearby me didn't have the same philosophy. These strangers found the need to talk. Get to know one another. For the first hour, there was a lot of chitchat. By hour five, the conversations had dried up and some jokester near the trunk decided to heckle the rest of us. "I've won three of these," he said smugly. "You all should just go home now."

As people began to drop out, the rest of us found more space on the car. Ways to stretch out, to get as comfortable as was possible in an uncomfortable situation. My competitor and I were directly opposite at one point, and I stared at him through half-shut eyes, trying to get a better read.

"You go to Lola's," he said at hour seven.

"I don't go there," I told him, "I work there."

"That's right," he said, agreeing with me.

And then nothing else. We were down to sixteen people by hour ten. Twelve people by hour fourteen. There was no more talking, just a lot of clock-watching. At hour twenty, the scowling teenager at the front was disqualified when a judge saw him popping an upper. No stimulants allowed, aside from coffee. And coffee screws you. Screws you seriously. Makes you have to pee all the time. Better to stay focused. To keep it all straight in your head.

"You're a musician," I said softly, finally placing him.

A nod, and his eyes held mine again. *It's you and me*, those deep blue eyes promised. It's always been you and me. Then nothing more until we hit the one-day mark. I had moved past feeling tired, reaching a different place, where sleep no longer felt necessary. I've deejayed before, done those sort of all-night stints that teach you what tired really means. Just like with hunger, there's a point where you can go beyond the fringe. Pass through and into a completely new zone. No longer tired, just wired. Crazy. Don't forget to hold the car.

"Oh, man," the lady closest to me yelled as the judge removed her. "I thought I was touching it."

"You were dreaming."

"Dreaming of winning."

Low chuckle from the rest of us. We'd never lose our grips. Just our senses.

"Guitar," he said as we paddled our way through the brain-daze of day two. "Guitar and vocals. My name's Adam. The band's called Gridlock." As he spoke, I realized not only had I heard of him, but I'd caught a show one time out on the strip.

"I'm Stella," I said, knowing as I spoke that the words sounded off. This was the wrong time and place for introductions. Still, I wasn't that surprised when he nodded and said, "Yeah, I know."

Before we could continue talking, the man hogging the trunk fell asleep and rolled off with a thud onto the tiled floor. This was the heavyset moron who had told the rest of us he'd won three vehicles in the past. But he wasn't going to win this one. The ass didn't wake up when the judges tried to move him. They dragged him off to a corner and let him sleep. A photographer covering the event for the *Weekly* took his picture. Now, *there* was something to send home to the family.

"Eyes on the prize," Adam whispered, closer to me somehow. Right at my side.

"Hand on the prize," I told him. "Eyes don't count."

"You make a mean margarita."

"That's my job."

"Could use one now," he said.

"A little lime, a lot of salt, that's the trick."

"Yeah," he nodded. "But I've never seen you drink one."

"Can't drink where you work."

He shook his head now. "No, that's not it. The customers offer and you decline. You're not into the mixed drinks. And you're not into mixing with the clientele."

I smiled. He had me pegged. "Tequila," I explained. "It doesn't need anything to make it drinkable."

"You know, I've seen him around," Adam told me.

"Him?" I asked, even though I had an instant feeling who he meant.

"Your man. Your ex. The fucking idiot."

"You've seen him where?"

"Clubs. You know the type. She's nothing compared to you. Some blonde wisp of a girl. She's got no stamina, no soul."

I swallowed hard and looked down at my feet. I'd wanted to hear that for a long time, but I'd wanted to hear those words from Justin.

"I mean it," he said next. "She's a poser. But you're real."

"And then there were five," said the judge. "Five people. Ten minutes to relieve yourselves. Be back here when the bell rings or don't bother coming."

Adam looked at me, and that glimmer of a grin touched his lips. Would I waste my precious minutes of freedom with him? Would *I* bother coming? That's what the look said. No. Not yet. I went outside for a break, not needing to relieve myself of anything but the glaze of fluorescents overhead, and I smoked my last cigarette at twilight. Coy, that's my method. Play coy, even when you've got no secrets left.

Back on the car, we were opposite again. Four of us. One lady hadn't returned from the rest break. "That's bizarre," the remaining teen said. "She was close. Why would she leave?"

"You never know," said the rumpled-looking businessman on the hood. "People seem to be one way, but then you learn they're different. Totally different." He sounded as if he were speaking from experience, and when I looked down at his hand, which was holding the car ever so lightly, I saw the mark around his finger where a wedding ring must once have been. Tanned skin around a pale white echo, a shadow of a ring.

"*She* was different," he said, feeling my eyes on his hand.

"Yeah," I found myself nodding. That was Justin, too. Seemed one way. Turned out to be another.

Then there was nothing. Silence except for the employees and photographers positioned around the car dealership. We'd become fixtures to the salespeople. They wandered by, offering a bite of a donut, telling us to keep our chins up. Salespeople are like chameleons. They can adapt to anything.

The next few hours seemed to go by quickly. And then I realized I'd been asleep on my feet, and my gothic musician had placed his hand on top of mine, holding it to the car. I could feel the cool metal of his silver rings against my fingers.

"Is that cheating?" I whispered, speaking as I woke up, feeling lightheaded and confused.

"It's break time again," he said, "come share a smoke." He tapped his chest pocket, indicating a full pack. I shook my head and left for the restroom. And in the small space, I stared at my expression. Seemed one way. Turned out different.

Back on the car, it was as if Adam had been in the bathroom with me.

"Not you," he whispered. "You're exactly how you appear. Aren't you?"

"What do you mean?"

"You can take it."

Our next break was ten minutes of sex. Ten minutes of the most intense sex I've ever had. Behind the dealership. Silver-white moonlight on us. His eyes on mine. I watched as he undid the polished buckle at the waistband of his faded jeans, stared as he pulled that leather snake of a belt free from the tattered loops. There was a nervous half-grin on my face. I could feel it, but I couldn't erase the expression. Excitement beat within me because of what that simple gesture meant. He had understood me easily. He wasn't just undoing his pants, he was getting out his tool, the favorite weapon of my choosing.

"Turn around," he whispered, his eyes holding me. And when I hesitated, his voice crooned, "Come on, girl. Come on, Stella—"

It happened fast after that. Belt off, and working in his hands. My palms flat on the brick wall, body erect. I stared at the chipped blue polish on my short fingernails, stared at the cracks in the bricks in the wall and the white mortar flaking away. Adam didn't have to say the words, but I heard them echoing in my head. "Take it."

The strokes were muted against my jeans. Too muffled by the tough fabric of my Levis and the gray panties beneath. That wasn't right. I needed to feel this. I needed to own the pain. My fingertips fumbled with the button-fly of my jeans, pulling them down past my knees, desperate for the hot flash of the leather against my naked skin. Needing that stripe of fire on my bare body before I could take his cock inside me.

He worked me just right. He used the belt like an extension of himself, and he heated me up all over. Melted my inner rocklike core until I felt the liquid pool within. The belt made a sound in the air before it connected with my skin. Just a whisper. Just a tease to let me know what was coming. My head lowered, my eyes closed, I did exactly what he said—I took it.

And when he was ready, and I was ready, he dropped the belt to the gravel-and-rock mixture below and pushed against me, his cock so hard, his body so warm. I sobbed into the freedom of being fucked like that. Losing myself in the pleasure of it all. There is a power in submission. There is a higher plane in accepting pain. The darkness unfolds inside me and all I feel is white, pure light.

Outside. So quick. Everything was right. Everything moved

together. I don't know how it happened. I just know that it was
right. I could feel his sharp exhale of breath on me as he brought
his mouth to the nape of my neck and bit me there beneath my
heavy hair. I gritted my teeth and arched into it, muscles in my
back tensed and alive, ready as I pressed my hips as tight as they
could go back against him. I felt his entire body slide into me,
holding me against the wall. Pinning me there. Our bodies fit
together in that puzzlelike way, and each place that was striped
along my ass and thighs seemed to burn into his skin. He murmured something to me just before he came, just before I came,
but I didn't hear him clearly. I couldn't have.

"The real prize." That's what he said. "You're the real prize."

Back on the car, I looked around, dazed. Me. Him. The businessman with the unfaithful wife. The teenager desperate for a car
to get away from his daily routine, to blaze off into the sunset
with his girl at his side. But at mid-morning, the teen crashed.
Literally. Falling onto the car as sleep took him away. He woke
as he hit the ground, and then shrugged and left the dealership.
Not saying good-bye. Not looking back.

Before the next break, the businessman started crying. Every
so often, tears would streak his face. But he wouldn't look at
anyone.

Nothing to lose, I thought again.

When the man's cell phone rang, all three of us jumped. He
reached for it, answered tersely, and then started to cry for real.
Taking his hand away from the car, he held on to the phone
with all ten fingers, gripping it to his ear. "Yes," he said, his
voice half a sob. "Yeah, of course." And then he was gone, too,
embarrassed, unwilling to stare back at me. He was giving her
another chance. That's what his slope-shouldered look meant.
He was giving her another chance because he couldn't stand the

pain of not having her. No reason for him to avoid my gaze. I'm as weak as the next broken-hearted lover. Would I have taken Justin back if he'd called? Can't tell you that one. He didn't call. Then all of a sudden, the dealership owner had his hand on my shoulder and was announcing me as the winner.

Where was Adam? Not here. Not there.

Keys thrust in my hand. Photos taken. Eyes blurred and blinking. Driving back home instead of walking, I couldn't believe this was me sitting in the shiny new car. At the light near my house, a Harley engine revved. I looked over at Adam, cracked my window, and asked what I'd wanted to ask for hours. "Why didn't you just let me fall asleep?"

"I didn't want the car."

Now, I stared into his eyes, waiting. "Why did you even try, then?"

"I saw you through the window. I didn't even know about the contest. I don't drive cars. I was coming home from rehearsal."

"Then you haven't slept in—" I couldn't count the hours. Days.

"Doesn't matter. You have to hold yourself together if you want to win."

The light went green, and as horns blared musically around me, he nodded for me to drive. I glanced in the rearview mirror and saw him following me to my apartment on the bike. We parked and headed in together, not bothering to walk down the hall to my bedroom. Not bothering even to speak. We pulled off our clothes, let them fall into dark puddles on the polished wood floor. He had me up against the wall in the living room, knocking stuff out of his way to get me how he wanted me. None of the rest of it mattered. Just connecting. Just feeling him on me again.

As his fingers parted my nether lips, searching out my wetness, I thought of how I'd climaxed alone before the contest.

Pushing myself to come again, and again. Now, my body responded as if I'd trained it to obey. I was so turned on, so ready. His fingertips brushed against my clit and I shuddered all over. His middle finger slipped deep inside my pussy as his thumb ran up and down my clit. Stroking. Soothing. Then his fingers worked together, spinning and spiraling, and I gripped onto his shoulders and shivered all over.

"Come for me, baby," he urged. "Come on, Stella—"

The white plaster wall was cold behind my back. His dreamy skin was warm to my touch. I was caught between the two sensations as he lifted me up, held me firmly and then slid me down on him. His eyes took me where I needed to go. They told me everything I had to hear. But that wasn't enough for him. He had to spell it out. He had to make it clear.

"I watched you for so long—"

"I didn't know."

"You were lost in your own world. But I saw you."

"Tell me," I begged, finding it hard to speak.

"You deserved better." He arched forward, driving inside me.

"Oh, god—," I whispered.

"You deserve this," he said, and I wrapped my legs around his bare waist, saw the colorful splash of tattoos I'd known would ride his chest, his arms. I closed my eyes as he leaned forward to bite my bottom lip. I felt his mouth on mine, rough and raw. The scrape of his three-day whiskers. The pain-pleasure of being taken. And finally I understood what he'd said as I came in his arms. Here it was when I hadn't even been looking. The real prize.

DOWN BELOW

Jean Roberta

D o your students like Poe?" asked my department head, Dr. Dorothy Kipperwell. She generally discouraged modern informality in the English Department, but she had asked me to call her Kip. "Do they understand the language?"

"They do when I explain it to them," I told her. "A lot of first-year students are still teenagers, Kip. They understand extreme emotions. Adolescence is a gothic period. Remember how it felt to be that age?"

I knew that I was peeking through the keyhole of a locked door. Kip was almost butch enough to pass for a man (suave, witty, and middle-aged, but with plenty of controlled aggression) and she had told me enough about her life to let me know that her youth had been hell. The classic teenage whine that "nobody understands me" had been very true for her. Her lonely coming-of-age had made her tough, discreet, and determined to survive on her own terms. Beyond all reason, I wanted to be the one person on earth who could pierce her armor and learn her secrets.

Kip smiled in a way that raised the fine hair on the back of my neck. I hoped my nipples weren't poking up shamelessly under my low-cut red silk top, and I didn't dare look down.

Kip looked coolly professorial in a navy-blue sweater and pants. She also looked amused. "You like to revisit that period, don't you, Athena?"

I felt my face grow hot. I reminded myself that Kip wasn't much older than I was (thirtysomething), or much taller. She was slim and muscular, but I'm slim, too. She had read a lot, of course, but that went with the territory; the same could be said about me. Like me, she had dark brown hair and eyes, although her eyes were smaller and looked more knowing than mine. Her hair looked short enough for the military, while mine flowed halfway down my back on occasions like this when it wasn't pinned up.

When we first met, Kip already knew that I had been a faculty brat all my life. She had heard of my parents: the historian Abraham Chalkdust and the linguist Anna Parle Chalkdust. If my pedigree impressed her, she didn't show it.

The quality in Kip that made me weak in the knees (even though I am not a weak person, as I reminded myself) seemed beyond my power to analyze. Telling myself that she was just an academic dyke like me didn't help me at all.

I ignored her last comment and plunged on with a discussion of my students, as though I were being interviewed for a job.

"They get the irony of the host's concern for his friend's health as the two men go deeper and deeper into the crypt of the family castle. Each time the host asks, 'Are you sure you don't want to go back?' the guest tells him to lead on. The guest ignores the cold, damp air of the place because he's drunk and trusting and curious. And he's dressed as a fool or jester, in a cap with bells. Students get it."

"It's one of your favorite stories, isn't it, Athena?" asked Kip. She was almost openly laughing at me. "This is interesting. What's your favorite part?"

I felt as if the answer must be written on my face, or maybe in the modest cleavage that showed above my neckline, the little valley that led directly to my heart. I knew that I couldn't ignore her question this time.

I nervously brushed the long hair out of my eyes and tossed it behind my shoulders before I realized how flirtatious this must look.

"That moment when the host chains his friend to the wall," I told her. I took a deep breath and let it out slowly. Kip's gaze dropped to my small, perky breasts, and her smile widened. "It's so intimate. He fastens his victim's wrists to bolts in the wall that have been used to secure captured enemies for centuries. Then the host chains his victim's waist. They must be physically close for that, and the fool doesn't fight back at first because he trusts his friend. It's only when he realizes that he's not going to be released that he struggles. 'For the love of God, Montresor!' he begs, but he gets no mercy."

I shifted my butt on Kip's sofa, and she looked down at my hips in sleek black pants.

"It's horrifying, of course," I said, "but think about it: Montresor wants to keep his old friend there forever, with the bones of his own ancestors. No one makes commitments like that anymore." I was trying to lighten the mood. I thought I sounded young and foolish.

"So you think the story has a homosexual subtext?"

"Yes," I told her, forcing myself to look into her shrewd chocolate-colored eyes. "No one names it, but it's there."

"And the act of chaining someone up seems erotic to you?" she demanded. "Or would you rather be the helpless victim?

The one who gets shackled or fettered in a dungeon by one who lured you down there by offering you something special?"

For the love of God! She had led me to this point in the conversation, and I had willingly followed. And now I couldn't find a graceful way to go back or get away. "Uh," I answered. "I'd like to be chained up." There. I had said it. "Not permanently, of course! Just for a while. By someone with better intentions than any of the maniacs in Poe's stories! I'd like to be locked up or tied up by someone who wants me. Alive. Not someone who wants me dead."

"Gotcha," grinned Kip. She didn't seem shocked at all.

Oh yes, I thought. *You get me, you read me, and now you know you can have me any time you want.* I was tempted to resign right then.

Kip had more to say. "You tend to run away if you're not tied down, don't you, babe? I bet you'd like me to chase you into a corner and wrestle you to the floor. You can get what you want, my dear, but you have to ask for it. That's the rule."

I really hadn't seen this coming. Two weeks before, Kip had seemed unusually friendly when I was the last guest to leave her house after a department party that she had put on as an icebreaker at the beginning of the fall semester. Once we were alone, her strong, graceful hands punctuated her comments with taps on my shoulders. While I was making a point about the transvestite heroines in Shakespeare's plays, she distracted me by stroking my hair. While showing me through her house, she led me by the hand. I secretly hoped that she was planning to throw me onto her vintage brass bed, but I couldn't be sure I was reading the signs clearly.

In any case, my common sense told me that getting sexual with my boss would be a really bad career move. My moist cunt was telling me other things.

Kip offered me a brandy and I accepted, but nothing she said or did was a clear proposition. Finally, I thanked her for a lovely evening and stood up to leave. She followed me to her front hallway, where she calmly pulled me into her arms as though she wanted to dance. Before I could react, she tipped my head back slightly and pressed her lips to mine. When I didn't resist, she slid her tongue into my mouth. *Yes!* I felt faint, but I didn't mind.

I could taste the wine she had drunk and the salty peanuts she had eaten. I could feel her heart beating beneath her small, hot breasts. I could feel my panties growing wetter, and I wondered if she could smell me. I breathed in her own clean but earthy smell as I moved my hips, hoping she found me irresistible.

Kip pulled her mouth away from mine, and smoothly pushed me away from her. "I'll see you at school on Monday, Athena," she smiled. I felt as if she had just poured ice water over me.

"Goodnight. See ya," I muttered. I grabbed my jacket and pulled it on while opening the front door, and rushed out into the darkness. I didn't want Kip to know how disappointed I was.

In the following weeks, I told myself that she had done the right thing, and that I should be glad to be working for someone who was ethical enough to protect me from my own reckless desire.

But my dreams were so lurid and drastic that I remembered them clearly while showering, dressing, and preparing myself for my audience of students. A few scenes even jumped into my mind's eye when I was driving to work or grading essays or exchanging small talk with a colleague: Kip beckoning me to kneel at her feet. Kip, dressed in black leather, pinching my bare nipples while discussing literature. Kip taking an old-fashioned wooden paddle off the wall of her office to use on my naked ass as I waited obediently on all fours. Kip approaching me with a scary grin that said that she wasn't violating my rights, she was giving us both what we wanted.

The best and worst scenes from the cinema of my imagination were full of restraining devices: Kip as a member of the Royal Canadian Mounted Police (and very handsome in the red serge uniform), pulling my hands behind my back (not gently this time), and securing them in metal handcuffs before pushing me into the backseat of a police cruiser to await further attention. Kip as a vaguely Shakespearian guard locking me, a mischievous and disheveled maid, into wooden stocks in a public square. Kip as a kidnapper, tying me up with rope before covering my eyes with a blindfold and my mouth with a gag, the better to spirit me away to her secret lair.

When the real Kip had invited me back to her house for a drink and a private conversation, I had ignored my common sense and said yes.

But now she had really gone too far. "I don't *run away*, Kip," I told her. "Jesus. I can take a hint. You told me you would see me later, at school. What was that about? I don't stay where I'm not welcome, and you almost pushed me out the door."

Kip's smile never wavered. "I did no such thing, Athena," she told me. "You assume far too much. You need to be taught a lesson. You haven't seen my basement yet, have you?"

"No," I sneered. "Is that where you keep the bodies?"

"Not yet," she replied calmly. "I've only lived here for a few months. But the house has a history. One of the previous owners was charged with cruelty to animals for keeping his dogs chained up in the basement. It's an easy thing to do, not only to animals."

Now here was the rub, so to speak: bondage could be abandonment and neglect based on contempt. It wasn't always loving entrapment, delicious conquest, security, and clear limits.

"The foundation of the house is made of limestone, very picturesque. Do you want to see it?"

"Yes, Kip," I told her, trying to breathe normally.

"I think you'd better call me Ma'am while you're here, my girl. That seems fitting, don't you think so?"

"Yes, Ma'am."

"Speaking of what fits, I want you to take off all your clothes before we go downstairs. I want to see you all over, and I want you to be in the proper frame of mind."

"Here?" I asked, somehow feeling hot and cold at the same time. "K—Ma'am?"

"Right here, baby," she smiled. "Take your time."

Trying not to blush, I raised my top up over my head, revealing my lacy black bra. "Nice contrast," she told me. "Your skin is so pale."

I managed to unhook my bra and drop it casually on my top. "Ahh," she told my hard red nipples.

I stood up to unzip my pants, and pulled down my panties at the same time, to get it over with. She licked her lips while looking at the dark triangle of my pubic hair. "You've never been shaved there, have you, girl?" she smirked.

"No, Ma'am."

Kip seemed to be imagining the slit between my legs surrounded by smooth pink skin, completely exposed to her gaze.

After taking off my socks and shoes, I stood naked for her inspection.

Kip walked around me as I stood still, trying not to shake or twitch. She gathered up my hair in one hand and lifted it off my shoulders and back, giving my sweaty skin a chance to breathe. "Stand straighter," she told me, trailing a hand down my back and leaving gooseflesh in her wake. "No, don't be stiff." She tweaked one of my nipples and ran a hand lovingly over my butt. She released my hair. "There's so much that could be done with you. Wait here." She disappeared into another room. I heard cupboard doors opening, and the clink of glass on wood.

Kip returned holding a glowing hurricane lamp. "This will help set the scene. Stone looks better in this light," she told me. "So does skin. You will look luminous as a damsel in distress." She turned off the electric light, plunging the room into darkness except for a circle of light around her lamp. "Follow me and watch your step," she ordered, pulling me by the hand.

The steps leading down to the basement were rough gray wood, and they creaked even under my bare feet. The basement in lamplight looked so large and ominous that the square shapes of a washer and a dryer in a laundry room suggested torture devices waiting to be used.

The gray stone of the foundation was only waist-high, with Gyprock above it. I wasn't sure what to expect, but I gasped when I saw two thick metal rings set into the wall, screwed into the wooden posts behind the Gyprock. Kip was obviously a more experienced player than I had ever guessed. With a pang of jealousy, I wondered whether she had invited other members of the department down here for an unusual interview or meeting or retreat. How unprofessional! *If she does this often*, I thought, *someone should report her to the administration.* My own hypocrisy stared me in the face, and I almost laughed aloud.

Kip set her lamp on the concrete floor. "Arms up, maiden," she told me. The thought of being at her mercy sent tingles straight to my clit, in spite of my common sense. I raised my arms, but my wrists didn't reach the iron rings until I stood on tiptoe.

"You're such a little thing," said Kip, making it sound like a compliment. "You need something to stand on." She pulled a sturdy wooden stand along the wall until it was directly under the rings. "Stand up," she told me. As I placed one foot on the stand, she helped by possessively grabbing my nearest buttcheek and giving me a hoist.

Standing on a wooden platform made me feel like a statue, and it brought my crotch closer to Kip's eye level. I raised my arms for her, and she secured my wrists to the rings in the wall by fastening them with velvet-lined cuffs that were surprisingly comfortable. *This isn't very medieval at all*, I thought before I could stop myself. Was I actually disappointed? I despaired for my usual common sense.

Kip seemed to read my mind. "Life in my dungeon can get a lot worse, girl," she warned. "I'm going easy on you because you're new here and I'm unreasonably fond of you. Best not to annoy me, eh?"

"I'd like to please you, Ma'am," I confessed. She smiled.

Kip wasn't finished. She pulled out a metal bar with velvet-lined cuffs at each end. *Fetters for my feet!* She locked one onto each of my ankles so that my legs were held apart. I could only guess why she didn't want me to close them. She stood back to admire her work, and decided that something else was needed.

"Chains," she said, as if to herself. She walked to a corner of the room, and pulled a length of chain from a large canvas bag. Standing in front of me, she was able to wrap one end around my neck, and wrapped the rest down over my back, several times around my waist, over my sensitive belly, and between my legs. Then she held her design in place by running two little padlocks through the links at my neck and belly.

The cold metal on my skin made me shiver, but the more I moved, the more it rubbed against my skin. Kip clearly enjoyed my dilemma, watching me discover the limits of my freedom.

I didn't want to risk knocking over the wooden stand because then I would be suspended from my wrists. I couldn't move very much without making things worse for myself.

"Get comfortable, my dear," grinned Kip. "You'll be here a long time." Panic raced through me before I reminded myself that she couldn't really keep me in her basement for days, weeks, or months. Someone would ask where I was. Wouldn't they?

"You need the cap and bells of a fool," she told me. "I interpret the word *cap* somewhat loosely. Not that they won't fit tightly." Suddenly she had two nipple clips in her hands, and she was reaching in between the length of chain over my chest to squeeze them onto my nipples. Each clip had three little bells dangling from it, and they jingled cheerfully with each breath I took.

Kip stepped back to admire her work. "Now," she addressed me seriously, "I won't gag you because I want you to talk. And I won't blindfold you because I want you to see. You should be grateful."

"Yes, Ma'am." The nipple clips were sending a message straight to my cunt. I felt as if my juice must be dripping onto the wooden stand, forming a puddle.

"Are you attracted to me, Athena?"

"Yes, Ma'am." *Duh. She just wants to rub it in*, I thought.

"Then why did you leave my house so rudely and abruptly last time?"

"You drove me away!" I protested. "You said 'I'll see you at work on Monday.' What could that mean except 'It's time to leave'?"

"Obviously, Athena," she pointed out mildly, "I expected to see you at school during the week regardless of what might happen between us in private on the weekend. You weren't planning to disappear into thin air, were you? If you wanted me, why didn't you say so?"

"I couldn't invite myself to spend the night with you!" I felt as if I could dissolve in tears like some doomed character in Greek mythology.

"Why not?"

"Because you could reject me; you could tell me how pushy and immature and unprofessional I was; you could tell me I wasn't worthy. You could even fire me on the spot. I didn't want to risk all that."

"Ah. But you, and women like you, expect me to make the first move and the last move and all the moves in between. With no risk or effort on your part. And you want to reserve the privilege of reporting me to the authorities any time you can't take the heat of your own desire. Yours, not mine. You don't want to risk losing your teaching career because it's what you love, but you'd be willing to force me out for life, and call me a monster, a Grendel from the lake of unwanted knowledge, to protect yourself. Wouldn't you?"

Kip really looked angry. *Shit.*

Tears stung my eyes, overflowed, and trickled down my cheeks. There was nothing I could do to stop them. "Oh, Kip, Ma'am, I really don't want to backstab you." *Liar*, I thought to myself. "I just didn't want you to turn me down. I couldn't stand it. I'd have to see you every day in the halls after that, and I just couldn't stand it. I would have to find a new job somewhere else, maybe not in a tenure track. You have to understand."

Kip looked coldly into my eyes. "Good start, girl. In earlier times, prisoners were usually tortured to get thorough confessions out of them. The whole truth and nothing but the truth. Very few people will tell it all if they're not under pressure."

She turned away from me, and walked into another room. In the split second after she disappeared from my sight, I realized that I would rather be physically hurt than left to languish down here alone until she might remember me, and decide to let me go.

Seconds and minutes ticked by as I heard muffled movements from another part of the basement.

After what I guessed was a twenty-minute absence, Kip came back to me. This time, she was wearing black leather pants, a black T-shirt and a black leather hood like a medieval executioner. And then I saw that she was holding a coiled bullwhip, a long and vicious leather snake.

I felt my blood actually running cold.

"Watch," she told me. She backed up, taking measured steps, then pulled the whip back over her head, and aimed it at the opposite wall. The whip cracked in the air before falling harmlessly to the floor. I was relieved that she hadn't knocked over the flickering lamp, but I was afraid my relief might be short lived.

"Please," I babbled, "please, Ma'am, don't hurt me with that thing. Or anything else you might have. I'll tell you whatever you want to know, but most people don't want the whole truth, you know?"

Kip smiled at me, and she looked beautifully at peace. "True enough, Athena, most people don't. This time, I think we'll just resolve the homosexual tension that appeals to you in Poe. Would you like that?"

My cunt felt like the inside of a volcano, if a volcano could want to be penetrated down to its lava-filled core. "Will you fuck me, Ma'am, please?" I begged.

"Gladly, my little slut. What would you like me to use?"

"Just your fingers this time, Ma'am. I want to feel you inside me."

Kip dropped the whip and strolled up to me, as though studying an exhibit in a museum. Without warning, she reached up and pulled the clips off my nipples. "Oh!" I burst out, as the bells jingled a wild tune.

And then she pressed her mouth against my wet, pungent bush and sent her tongue on a scouting trip to find my clit. She sucked hard as two of her fingers slid into me with the greatest of ease. She tickled my cervix and stroked my inner folds and harassed my G-spot until I felt as if I might explode. "Come, baby," she told me. "I want you to come for me."

"Ohhh!" The sound of my own voice bounced off the basement walls as I breathed in the smell of kerosene and reveled in the feeling of cool metal sliding over my skin.

"Good girl," purred Kip. "I'll let you down now, so I can hold you close to me. But you have to promise not to sneak away."

That was probably the easiest promise I ever made.

BETTY'S
BOTTOM

Michael Hemmingson

I knew Betty from the blogosphere. I knew she was twenty-nine, lived here in L.A., was into pain, worked as a submissive in a dungeon, and constantly craved a Jamba Juice.

One time she wrote in her blog: *If anyone out there brings me a Jamba Juice to work, they'll get something special.*

I wrote: *I'd bring you one every day.*

Her user handle was SoozyQ, Betty was her pro name, and Elaine (apparently) her true name. She seemed obsessed with images of women in uniform and pictures of Edward Norton in *American History X*. For several months we exchanged blog posts about sex and drugs and loneliness. She kept late hours until sunrise like I did. One night she wrote she was upset because an ex-boyfriend had posted pictures of his dick entering her cunt on the Internet, and she gave me the link. She told me how one night someone gave her what she thought was XTC but it was actually acid and she had to work in that state of mind. I told her about the massive amount of 'shrooms I'd been taking lately and she said she didn't like 'shrooms *because they make me see witches*. When asked what was the nicest gift anyone could give her, she replied: *A family and a home*.

That was a good answer.

Since joining the blog universe, I've struck up about a dozen online "relationships" with women all over the country, from ages seventeen to forty-seven, ranging from flirtatious emails; cybersex on Instant Messenger; late-night phone calls when their husbands, boyfriends, or parents are asleep; to some of them flying, driving, or taking Amtrak into San Diego for a weekend to see if there is any chemistry "in the meat world," as they say in the vernacular. Usually, it's awkward and doesn't work out...so I often suggest before they make the trip, that upon meeting in person we immediately jump into a quick, hard fuck. Why not? That's why they're coming to see me, and sex will be on our minds the whole time—you know, who should make the first move, will a move be made, will there be sex, will the sex be good? If the sex is taken care of right away, then there won't be all that tension and anticipation and we'll both know if the sex is good and if we should continue with the visit as friends or mere tricks.

So I was a little nervous about meeting Betty in L.A. and she said she was, too, though I wondered about that since our pre-arranged get-together was going to be brief and contrived. She was a professional, after all, and I was going to pay her for the time at the going rate plus a tip, and I knew there wasn't going to be any actual sex involved.

This was also going to be a new experience for me, dropping into an S/M dungeon. I felt better that I was going to be with a woman whom I'd at least communicated with and knew a little bit about, rather than a complete stranger.

I've never been into the BDSM or D/s scene much; the lifestyle fascinates me and I like the clothing and gear and attitude in an academic sort of way, but it simply doesn't turn me on, nor is it something I pursue with the kind of passion that many in the scene do with almost religious fervor and intent.

I set up a Sunday appointment with Betty at 1:30 p.m. The dungeon was located across the street from LAX in a warehouse zone on South La Cienega Boulevard. If you didn't have the address and didn't know what it was, you'd never have guessed such a place of business was among the rows of bland, cookie-cut rectangular buildings that looked like they were built in the 1950s. The windows were tinted and there was an American flag in front of the place in question. I was told there was a discreet back entrance for clients who didn't want to be seen going in or out but I didn't care; I pressed the intercom button, said I had an appointment, and was buzzed inside.

The lobby was appropriately dark; a fat, greasy man in a pastel shirt who looked like the clichéd smut peddler sat behind a wooden desk. He looked me up and down and seemed bored. On a leather couch to my left was a woman with short hair and chewing gum and wearing a pink teddy; at the desk to my right sat a short blonde woman at a computer, doing something on the Internet. I knew this was Betty; she was often online at work and I recognized her from some photos I'd seen: long, thick, curly hair; round face; slightly chubby body; big breasts and innocent-appearing blue eyes.

I had two Jamba Juices with me, orange and a berry flavor. She chose the orange and I had the berry.

She was shy and had a soft, high-pitched voice. She didn't look me in the eye when we shook hands, nor when she gave me a tour of the facility. But maybe this is what submissives are supposed to act like, what did I know?

This dungeon was a 7,000-square-foot warehouse split up

into various themed rooms. The Bastille Room, a jail cell with a rack; the Elizabethan Room, soft and pink and good for tickling; the O Room, minimally decorated with plain white walls and some hard-core torture devices; the Mae West Room, for clients who liked to cross-dress, and that door was closed; Windsor Hall was a classroom setting with half a dozen student chairs, a teacher's desk, and a chalkboard; the Interrogation Room was set up for some hard-core action and had quite the fascist feel; Windsor Stables was the pony-training area and the biggest—it was like a studio soundstage or small theater.

"Movies could be made here," I said.

"Oh, several have been," Betty said, looking at the floor.

"What kind?"

"What kind do you think?"

"S/M, I guess."

"And some hard-core porn."

I chose the Marquis de Sade Room, second biggest to Windsor Stables; everything in it was black or purple and there was a rack, cross, shackles, torture tower, and a suspended cage connected to the ceiling and tracks, so it could be pushed from one side of the room to the other. I chose this room because it had a large, comfy couch with pillows. I would have wanted Windsor Hall, the classroom, if Betty had been wearing a schoolgirl outfit (she was in white lace), so I could be the perverted teacher and she the naughty nymph coed.

We went up front and told the fat man which room. "How long?" he asked me. I said, "Half an hour," and he said, "A hundred dollars." I already knew what the prices were going to be; an hour went for a hundred and sixty and I almost took that but this was my first time; what if I got bored?

I gave the guy a hundred-dollar bill and Betty took me to the equipment room, where I had the choice of dozens of whips, paddles, leather masks, and so on. I had no idea what to do so I went for the obvious: handcuffs. I grabbed some clothespins too because I remembered a blog post of Betty's about how she liked them clamped on her nipples. Then I randomly grabbed a paddle. "Ohhh," said Betty, "that one's the worst. It's so hard."

It was a pretty heavy paddle and looked like it was made of walnut.

In the room, I said, "Okay, look, I told you I'm pretty cherry to all this so I have to say, I don't know what to do."

"Well, it's all about fantasy," Betty said.

"But what are the do's and don'ts?"

"There's no nudity, you can't touch me on my private parts underneath my bra and panties, and there's no exchange of bodily fluids."

"Let's keep it simple," I said. "What if I give you a spanking?"

"Okay. Where?"

"The couch."

I sat on the couch and she stood in front of me, looking quite demure.

"And I want you to call me Daddy the whole time," I told her.

"Daddy," she said, "lift up my skirt."

I did. She was wearing a white thong. She lay down across my lap. Her hair smelled like shampoo and I could also smell her pussy.

"Daddy, I've been so bad."

"Yes," I said, "you have," and I began to spank her, first on the left asscheek and then on the right; back and forth like that, soft at first because I knew enough to know that you did this lightly and built your way up. Her ass was big and round and pink and her flesh jiggled.

I've had plenty of girlfriends who liked the occasional spank-ing—a smack on the rear while I fucked them in the ass or some playful stuff to get them excited, but I'd never done an actual session like this before.

As I spanked her harder, my hand began to hurt so I switched to the paddle. When I took my first hard swing, the hard wood against her butt made a reverberating sound in the de Sade Room; she tensed up and hissed and I saw that her asscheek was bright red.

"I'm sorry," I said. "Too hard?"

"Not at all, Daddy."

"Harder?"

"If you wish, Daddy. Hurt me good, Daddy."

So I did...and I got into it. It took me maybe fifteen minutes to get into what this was all about, and when I did, I loved it. Her butt was turning black and blue and she was crying out and squealing and sometimes her body went completely stiff and she'd shudder. But in my mind, she was no longer a woman I knew from the Internet whom I was paying to do this to; she was Tori, who had walked out of my life four months ago, who'd left me alone and now refused to see or talk to me. Yes, she was Tori and I was punishing Betty (Tori) for what Tori had done, for hurting me: I was hurting her back. *You bitch,* I thought as I slammed the paddle down, *you cunt, you piece of worthless shit,* and I guess I got too carried away because Betty said, "Okay, okay, that's too hard, not that hard, Daddy."

Her ass was completely red, with several black-and-blue spots. Her body was shaking and covered in sweat. I was hot and sweating too. I felt bad that maybe I'd gone too far, so I rubbed her back and stroked her hair and ran my fingers up and down her legs; my hand moved between her legs, keeping above the thong panties, and she was wet—I could feel it, see it, and smell it. She was enjoying this, I guessed. She said, "Give me some more, Daddy."

So I did, but not too hard; I couldn't get back into the fantasy that I was punishing Tori so I pretended I was her evil Daddy and she was my daughter and she was a bad girl and I was going to have sex with her all night long. I told her this and she said, "Oh yes, Daddy, I want you to fuck me tonight, I want my Daddy's dick inside me because I'm such a *bad little slut.*"

"You are bad," I said and began to use the paddle harder to keep my mind off my hard-on that was pressing against her stomach and that she apparently knew was there because she began to grind her torso into my crotch.

The buzzer went off; our half hour was up. I could have gone for another thirty minutes but this was good enough. Betty stood up; her makeup was smeared and tears had run down her bright pink face.

"Okay?" I asked.

She smiled. "I would've been more verbal but I was just trying to survive that paddle. Oh, man," she said, lifting her skirt and looking at her backside in the mirror on the wall, "my ass is gonna be a mess tomorrow."

I got up and we both grabbed some cheap motel-style towels to wipe off sweat and tears. We stopped and looked at each other and then hugged.

I gave her a fifty-dollar bill as a tip, hoping it was a generous one.

I then gave her a kiss and she closed her eyes and smiled.

"Thanks for the new experience," I said.

"Come back again."

"I will."

"Maybe get a second girl, double your fun."

The other girl was asleep on the couch in the lobby. The fat man nodded at me. I walked out of the dungeon like I was being released from county jail, and I noticed that the sun was very bright. I didn't feel dirty like I thought I would. I felt—fuck if I know—cleansed in a way. I felt less angry. I may have even been a little happy.

MASTER OF TECHNOLOGY

Vanessa Evans

Last night, I got a spanking. A serious spanking. One that I'm still feeling today. My pretty, heart-shaped bottom is still a pale pink hue all over, faded down from the dark purplish color it reached last night. But I'm not complaining. In truth, aside from always being in the mood for a good old-fashioned spanking, I *deserved* the punishment. I hadn't learned Mac OS-X Tiger yet, and I'd promised Morgan that I would go online and study the information on Apple's website. In fact, I'd been promising for months to upgrade. But the thing is, I'm perfectly comfortable with my current system. Why make a change if everything is working? That's my philosophy.

"Lazy," Morgan said menacingly, "is different from comfortable." As he spoke, he slowly lowered the zipper running the length of my cashmere turquoise sweatshirt. His fingers casually stroked my small, firm breasts through my thin white T-shirt. Immediately, my rosy nipples grew hard and erect, and I had a difficult time thinking up an excuse for my misbehavior. When

I get turned on, my mind goes hazy, and when Morgan touches me like that, all thoughts leave my head. As his fingers tweaked my nipples even tighter, I started to make a soft moaning sound. But Morgan was looking at me with a fierce expression on his striking face, obviously expecting some sort of explanation.

"I like the way my computer works," I finally responded, sullenly, unable to hide the defiant tone in my voice, even though I knew that being flippant with Morgan would make my punishment more severe.

"You're just plain lazy," he said again. His dark green eyes burned with a fiery glow. "If it weren't for me, you'd still be using those huge floppy discs from the eighties."

"That's not fair," I told him, raising my arms over my head so he could pull off my soft white T-shirt. "I was a teenager in the eighties."

"Right. You were too busy listening to Madonna to learn how to turn on a computer. But you know what I mean," he insisted, undoing the clasp of my white lace bra and sliding the silky garment free from my body. Morgan thinks that a true punishment should always be delivered in the nude. Whenever he disciplines me, he strips me first. That is, unless we're outdoors, and he has to move quickly.

"Turn this way, Vanessa," he hissed under his breath, and I hurried to obey, offering him my backside so that he could unzip my short pleated skirt. "You're a Luddite," he continued, darkly. "You never want to accept any sort of modern change."

"How can you say that?" As I spoke, I looked down at my skirt, puddling in a ripple of blue and green plaid at my feet, rather than looking at Morgan. My dark bangs fell into my eyes. "I've got an iBook, for god's sake," I muttered, half under my breath.

"But you use it like a typewriter!" This was his ultimate insult, and I felt myself blush. He was right. I hardly know how to use any of the various intricate programs on my computer that are designed to make my life easier. I only know how to open new files and print. As I had nothing to say in my self-defense, I remained quiet as he slid off my white satin panties. He waited impatiently for me to step out of them, and I did so quickly. Now, I was entirely nude, save for my ponytail holder, which Morgan let me keep in. He likes to use my long, dark ponytail as a handle sometimes, keeping me still while he spanks me or fucks me.

"Bend over," he said, his voice so stern that I almost came right on the spot. I love it when Morgan talks to me like that, and he knows it.

"Yes, Sir." I started to move toward the couch across the room, thinking that's where he wanted me. I've been in spanking position over our couch countless times.

"No, baby. I want you to bend over the desk and hold yourself steady. This time, it's going to hurt." Then, almost as an afterthought, "You've got to learn somehow."

I gritted my teeth and waited for the first blow. Of course, Morgan let me wait. He never starts a spanking right away. After stripping my clothes off completely, he always takes his time, making me tremble in anticipation. My whole body tenses, readying itself for the surprising burst of pain to start. My mind takes a fantasy trip, remembering previous times when he's spanked me, recalling both the pain and the echoing pleasure that every spanking brings me. It's only when I finally start to relax that he begins.

This time was no different. The muscles in my arms were locked tight and my head lowered to my chest, but he didn't pull his battered leather belt free and let the first blow land on my bare ass until I started to relax my grip. When he started, he moved quickly. The belt uncoiled in a heartbeat and then he was on me. At the initial contact, I squealed out loud. The sensation was intense—raw leather meeting naked skin—but not so intense that I couldn't stand it. I knew how wet I was even now, because I could see the shiny evidence of my arousal already making the tops of my thighs slick.

"Count for me, Vanessa," he insisted. "Count them out."

"Yes, Sir," I murmured softly. "That's one."

"Good girl."

Somehow, I knew there'd be ten. Ten blows for failing to master Mac OS-X 10.4.3 Tiger. That seemed an even punishment. Morgan may be stern, but he's fair. Ten lines on my skin that I could admire later, stroking one after the other while staring over my shoulder at my well-chastised reflection in the full-length bathroom mirror. Morgan always leaves marks to remind me. He knows that no matter how much I might protest, how much I might squirm or swear or stamp my feet, I love the memory marks he gives me. I use those marks as masturbatory fuel, fiercely fingering myself and replaying the spanking over and over in my mind for days afterward. The reality is that Morgan loves to spank me as much as I crave his firm hand or his strict belt on my ass. In this way we're a perfect match, even if I am a failure at staying current with technology.

"If you miss a number, we start over," Morgan said. "We go back to one, no matter what." He explains the rules to me before every single spanking, even though we've gone through this scenario countless times. I could recite the rules for him by heart by now. But he's a kind disciplinarian in that way. He never tries to catch me unawares.

The second blow lined up right beneath the first. I could feel my ass smarting, and I was shocked at how hot my skin was after only two strikes. I knew that I'd be practically on fire by ten. I was sure of it. But that was Morgan's point, after all. To teach me a lesson, as well as to turn me on. I wondered if he'd make me cry this time. I didn't know. I can never tell. The one thing I could be sure of was that he would make me come. But I also knew that a climax wouldn't happen until I'd taken the complete punishment. Morgan is fair in that way, too. There is no cheating when he's delivering a spanking. No getting out of the actual punishment portion of our play.

"Count," he demanded, reminding me, and I realized that I was so lost in my thoughts, I'd already failed him. "Two," I said quickly. "Two, Sir," and Morgan stroked my ass with his hand and then squeezed me tight. "Behave, kiddo," he said. "You don't want to make me really angry."

Oh, but didn't I? He was wrong about that, because pushing Morgan to his limits is all part of the fun. If I failed to obey, he might get his polished silver handcuffs out of his top dresser drawer. He might cuff me in the center of our bed and do all sorts of twisted and kinky things to me that would make me come even harder than a simple spanking. In the past, when I've gotten out of hand, he's used nipple clamps on my perky tits, and clothespins on my plump pussy lips. He's inserted a well-lubricated vibrator deep into my dripping wet pussy and a sweetly rounded butt plug in my haughty ass. Would he pull out all the stops today? Only if I tested him.

Morgan's belt landed a third time, and I yelped out, "Three!" Then he let it strike me two times in rapid succession and I stumbled over the words "Four," and "Five," trying to keep still for him, trying not to flinch too badly. My voice shook as I spoke, and I could hear the tears waiting to come out. But as much as I love to test Morgan, he also loves to test me. He took a break for a moment after the fifth blow, and I was aware of how completely aroused I was. My pussy was tightening and opening automatically, waiting for the moment of total release. I could practically taste how good this was going to feel. With the spark of pain still alive in my skin, my cunt swam with pleasure.

When my juices continued to rain down my thighs, and when Morgan didn't land the next blow, I couldn't help myself. I brought my fingers between my pussy lips and lightly touched my clit. I didn't mean to. It was as if my brain had no control whatsoever over my body. I *had* to touch my clit. A light little touch. Almost a tickle. And that's all it took to make me come. While my body shook all over, Morgan said nothing. He carefully stroked my stinging asscheeks, and his touch there, gentle and sweet, extended the climax for me. My whole body shivered as the power of my pleasure flooded through me. My free arm remained locked on the edge of the desk, but my back and ass and legs shuddered with the violent contractions. I groaned and closed my dark brown eyes, momentarily forgetting that I was being punished. But as soon as my orgasm subsided, Morgan's demeanor changed. What I'd done was strictly against the rules. When Morgan is spanking me, I must obey his rules. No flinching. No touching. No coming.

No *nothing* unless he gives permission.

Without a word, he caught me up in his strong arms and carried me down the hall to our bedroom. His clothes felt alien against my sticky, naked skin. He was still wearing his oxford button-down shirt and his faded khakis, while I was nude and glistening, my only decoration the marks he'd already left on my supple ass.

In total silence, I was thrown in the center of the bed, facedown, and I trembled all over while waiting to see what would happen next. Would he break out the handcuffs? The crop? The toys? I heard him rustling in the drawer behind me, and after several moments he came forward with a lush purple velvet blindfold. I felt the velvet brush my face and my heart raced even more ferociously in my chest. He slid the mask into place easily, and then all was darkness.

"Can you see, Vanessa?" he murmured, his voice closer to my ear than I had expected.

I shook my head, then quickly responded, "No, Morgan. I can't see at all."

Next, he gripped my wrists together and in moments I found myself cuffed to our big brass headboard. Automatically, I tested my bindings, heard the clink of the chain he'd run through the curlicues of our headboard, and understood that I wasn't going anywhere for a while. Not until Morgan was done with me, anyway. But in the back of my mind I knew that I didn't want to go anywhere. I was secure in my belief that this scene would play out to my utmost pleasure—in spite of any pain I might have to absorb along the way. Or, to be honest, because of it.

Now, I heard the unmistakable sounds of my man moving to the side of the bed. He didn't say a word. I supposed he was watching me, and I tried to behave for him, tried to make my body stay entirely still in the center of the bed, tried my very best not to squirm. But then I heard it: the sound of his crop hitting the naked palm of his hand, and I shuddered involuntarily. He was going to give me the five final strokes with *that*—and this realization made me turn my face toward his and start to beg.

"I'm sorry—"

"You will be—"

"Morgan, I mean it."

"So do I, baby," he said. "So do I."

Tears started to run under the mask and down my face, raining onto our satiny comforter, and he hadn't even landed the first blow with the crop. That's how much power that simple tool has over me. Even the mere thought of it makes me tremble.

"You know you deserve this, Vanessa," he said softly, and I had to nod in agreement. Yes, I deserved this. And if I were to look deeper into myself, I knew something else: I wanted it. More than anything, I wanted to feel the sting of the crop on my already seriously smarting buttocks. Wanted this punishment to be one that I'd remember. Because the truth is that I need this sort of situation in order to bring me to my highest point—I need Morgan to crop me, to take me to a heightened place of extreme arousal that only the mixture of pain and pleasure will bring.

"How many, baby?" Morgan murmured.

I could answer that quickly, but I didn't want to.

"How many?" he repeated, his tone darker still.

"Five." My voice was hushed and contrite.

"That's right, baby. And remember. You count them out for me."

The first stroke landed almost immediately after his words stopped. I sucked in my breath in a great hungry rush, and then said, "One." Oh, god. One. That's all it was. I had four to go, and already my poor bum was on fire. Morgan landed the second right after, and then the third, so that my body shimmied on the bed in an almost indecent dance, trying to absorb the pain and trying to accept it. Morgan moved forward then, I felt his weight on the bed, and suddenly his fingertips were between my legs, probing. He came away with the succulent wetness that awaited him, and then he moved higher on the bed and smeared my juices along my own lips. I stuck my tongue out automatically to taste myself, and then Morgan kissed me, licking off the rest of my own honeyed juices.

"See?" he said, his voice a husky whisper. "See how your body responds?"

I nodded. I did see. No matter how much I try to tell myself that I don't need this sort of discipline in my life, my body never lies.

"Prepare yourself, baby," Morgan said, standing once again. The crop flashed down. I could hear the hiss of the air, feel the wind that it created before the beastly weapon struck blow number four. I managed to squeak out the number and my body stiffened, waiting for the final blow. Morgan let me wait. I heard a new sound now, and I tried to figure out what was going on. Then as I heard the clink of change hitting the floor, I realized Morgan was undressing. He was planning on being naked for blow number five. My body thrilled inside at what that meant. He was almost ready to fuck me.

Almost.

I could imagine him pacing naked back and forth along the side of the bed. I could visualize his cock standing up straight and tall, as if this part of him wanted a look at me as well.

And then he struck.

Number five was the fiercest cut yet, and I yelled when Morgan landed the blow in a crisscross motion that covered the previous four. Then quickly he was in motion again, on the bed behind me, using his hands to part my cheeks and sliding his cock deep into my pussy. There was no need for any other foreplay than what we'd just done. No need for any lubrication but my own.

As Morgan fucked me, he pulled off my blindfold, and I blinked at the bright lights, awash in the sensation of being cuffed to the bed while fucked from behind. I squirmed forward, gripping the brass railings with my hands to keep myself steady as Morgan continued to pound into me. He'd gotten so hard from spanking and cropping me, it felt as if he were fucking me with a steel pole. But even as he thrust in repeatedly, he didn't leave me wanting. Knowing exactly the touch I like, Morgan slipped one hand beneath my body and began to skate his fingertips along my swollen clit. The pleasure that came from his touch was almost overwhelming. I yelped at the first stroke of his fingers there, and then relaxed into the movement. I knew he was going to make me come, but he seemed determined to keep me teetering on the edge until he was ready to climax as well. As soon as I reached a point where I was moaning in pure bliss, he backed his fingers off of my hot button and began making slippery circles around my clit instead.

Finally, when I thought I could take the suspense no longer, he pressed three fingers right against my clit and I screamed out as I came, shaking the entire bed with my still-cuffed hands.

"That's it, baby," Morgan sighed into my hair. "That's right."

He bucked hard and came right after me, groaning as he shot deep inside of me. His body shuddered all over with the power of his orgasm. I'd already had one release, while bent over the desk, but this was his first climax of the evening and his body was wracked with the pleasure of it. Then, with a sigh, he pulled out and reached for the handcuff key that dangled on a pink shoestring from the bedside lamp. With a bemused smile he unlocked the cuffs and then grabbed me once again in a sticky and satisfied bear hug. I returned his smile, but I couldn't help thinking to myself that we'd be back in this same situation before too long.

At least we will when Morgan finds out that I've secretly held on to my Walkman. I was supposed to have mastered my iPod weeks ago.

BAD DOGGY

Julia Moore

Late last night, I told him what I wanted. It was dark. The type of dark that you don't talk about when daylight shines through your windows. The kind of dark dreams you're not even supposed to have when you're the fresh-faced girl that I am. Sweet and innocent. Pure and unmarked. Christ, people are so fucking dense. They get lost on surfaces. They look at me and see all of the light and cheerful adjectives found on your average Hallmark card. But they don't see the real thing. They don't see the flaws or the bruises, or the desperate fantasies. Nobody sees the real me except Justin.

"You want to what?" my boyfriend asked, one strong, tattooed arm tight around my slender body. And when I didn't immediately repeat myself, he insisted, "Say it again."

"I can't."

"You'd better—"

"I want to be your pet—"

"You *are* my pet," he assured me, nuzzling his face against the back of my neck. His full lips parted, teeth bared, ready to bite.

"I'm not talking about being your *good* pet," I told him, eyes straight ahead, staring at the red-painted wall in front of me, focused on it so I wouldn't have to look over my shoulder and see his expression change. "Not your sweet kitten. Not your puppy dog."

"Then what?"

"I want to be—"

"Say it."

"I want to be your bad doggy."

I felt him stiffen against me. In a single, silent frame, I felt his cock harden, felt his whole body change. From boyfriend to Master in just one breath. He sighed, and I felt that warm rush of air against the nape of my neck, and then I sighed, too, with the relief of confessing. After that, everything happened so quickly that the actions were difficult for me to process. He was moving, standing at my side by the bed, and he was positioning me in the very center of our mattress, on my hands and knees, head up, shoulders back. I moved automatically, accustomed to obeying, but even so, I knew that this was different.

Justin admired my stance, and I felt more naked than I ever had before. The way his eyes roamed over my figure, as if he were a judge at one of those high-class dog shows, and I was just another fancy bitch in heat.

"You look good, Celia," he said before turning away and rummaging through the contents of my dresser, searching for something. I should have guessed what he wanted, but I didn't. He came back with a rhinestone-studded pink leather collar, which he attached as tightly as it would go around my neck.

"Now, bark like a dog for me."

"A little dog or a big dog?" I said, and I giggled nervously, even though I knew how serious this whole thing was. I'd told him. I'd confessed completely. Now, he was giving me what I wanted. I should have been in the part already, not outside looking in, which is how I felt. Poodle-blonde hair tousled up in a high ponytail. That cute little collar around my slender throat.

"Your choice," he said magnanimously. "Whatever works for you."

I thought about it for a moment. But he was giving me too much freedom of choice. My thoughts wandered. What type of canine was I most like? A fiery-tempered dalmatian? A sweet-natured retriever? A carefully clipped high-end bitch with a haughty little wiggle? My golden-blonde bangs fell dramatically over my forehead, and Justin sweetly pushed the lock out of my eyes so that he could clearly see my face.

"I don't think I can—," I said, even though I heard the barking sounds in my head. The rough, low growls of a purebred. *Make me do this,* I wanted to tell him. *I can't do it on my own. You do it for me.*

Justin didn't say a word. Not one word. He simply waited.

I closed my eyes and tried to obey. But I couldn't. Here it was. Just the scene I'd begged him to give me. I was a bad doggy. And I couldn't even bark for my Master.

"You've already got the collar on," he said, his blue eyes shining as he tricked one finger beneath the thin leather band around my throat, "and you like wearing a leash when we go to S/M clubs, so what's the fucking problem?"

I didn't know. I just couldn't do it. I thought back to my high school days, when I'd gone with friends to a rowdy after-school football game. Everyone rooted wildly for the team, screaming whenever we scored a point, but I simply mouthed the cheers, unable to join in the chorus of happy yells. Even today, I find it difficult to raise my voice in public, and sometimes waiters have a hard time hearing me when I place an order.

"A simple yip," he tried next, climbing between my spread thighs and beginning to lick slowly up the inside of my legs. His ginger-red goatee tickled my skin in the most delicious manner. His tongue took tremulous, circuitous journeys on its way northward.

"Come on, Celia," he urged. "Come on, little puppy. Wouldn't you do anything you could to turn me on, Celia?"

Justin always knows how to bring me pleasure—pleasure that only comes from playing the most dangerous types of bedroom games. He's the one who turned me on to being tied down; the sole boyfriend who ever read the deep, dark wish in my gaze to be a submissive. Others pegged me for a sweet thing, a vanilla chicklet who wouldn't dare break a boundary. Not Justin. He raises the bar each time we fuck, and then he brings it right down on my naked hide, marking me as his own.

"Woof," I said, and I would have collapsed upon myself in helpless giggles if I wasn't so incredibly nervous. As it was, my body shook dramatically, but that might have been because Justin had reached my clit and was now centered on it with the full attention of his lips and tongue. He made slow, sloppy circles around and around, and I raised my hips up to meet his angelic mouth.

"Woof, woof," I tried.

"No, you're not into it," he critiqued, lifting up to look at me. I saw the shimmering gloss of my sex juices spread on his skin, shiny in the light. "You call yourself an actress?"

"I've never played an animal before."

"But you've played a whore. You've played a coke addict and a schoolteacher and an alien princess. All that's required of you is a little imagination. So what's the real problem?"

I didn't have an answer.

"You know what happens to naughty puppies, don't you?" Justin said.

Jesus, no, I didn't. But the way he spoke gave me an instant idea of how the night might wind up. I suddenly foresaw what lay in my immediate future. Embarrassment. Arousal. Pain and pleasure. My face pressed into my own filth. And all because I was being disobedient to my Master.

"Bad doggy," Justin said, making a *tsk-tsk* sound with his tongue on the roof of his mouth. My heart did a flip-flop. My stomach clenched. I felt tears come to my eyes, because he knew. This is what I wanted. This is what I'd asked him for. "Such a bad little doggy—" He reached up to tug on the collar around my throat, emphasizing his words with each firm pull. Why was I suddenly so wet?

"Please," I murmured. "Tell me what happens to naughty puppies."

"Try me," he said, "keep pressing my limits and you might just find out." And now he rolled me over in the bed. I heard the metallic click as he attached a leash to the collar, and then he was pulling back on the leather, forcing me to lift my head high. The fine muscles in my back tightened as I arched up. I could see my reflection in the round, gilded mirror over our bed, could see Justin take his position behind me. He was going to fuck me doggy-style. How appropriate was that?

"Head up," he insisted, and I worked even harder to keep my balance and stay tall and firm. "Belly up," he said next, tapping his fingers along my stomach. I took a deep breath, feeling my body respond to his commands. "Now, tail up," he said, a smile in his voice. "Come on, Celia. Tail up—"

I shifted my hips, raising an imaginary tail high into the air. Then I gave my hips a subtle swivel, as if wagging my tail back and forth. In my head I saw myself as "best in show."

"You're going to bark," he assured me now. "As I fuck you, I want you to bark."

I could feel tears streaming down my cheeks. This was beyond mortifying. How was I supposed to make a sound like a dog? Forget what I'd told him. Forget what I'd asked for, a scenario that I'd spent years coming to. Forget it. All bets off. My brain couldn't compute.

"You understand, don't you, Celia?" he murmured as he slid his hard, dreamy cock between my thighs. He'd gotten incredibly aroused simply from our bizarre conversation. That should have told me something. When I didn't answer, he pulled on the leash again, jerking my head up, and I nodded quickly. But that wasn't the type of response he was looking for. His hand came down hard on my rear, and I contracted instantly around his cock at the stinging sensation.

"Bark for me, baby," Justin insisted. "Be a good doggy, just this once."

I closed my eyes. I tried to see the image in my mind. This is a trick I do at any audition; picture myself in the role. Lose myself firmly so that the "me" that is Celia Martin dissolves, to be replaced with the character I am going for. But now my character was a dog. Could I go that route? As I'd done before, I worked to get a feel for what type of mutt I'd be. A midsized pup, I decided. Well groomed. Well cared for. With a low voice and a high spirit. A dog who would play Frisbee in the park. Who would chase the neighbor's pissy white Persian cat up a tree. Who would bring the newspaper up to her Master, but not release it upon request. A playful bitch, one that wasn't completely obedient—not out of disrespect, but out of sheer willfulness.

"Bark," Justin said, his cock driving hard, his hand slipping around my waist to find my clit. This was the missing link, the piece that I had needed to locate my center.

It wasn't a *woof, woof,* this time. Not a *bark,* not a *yip.* I opened my eyes, met his gaze in the mirror, tossed my long turbulent mane of gold hair free from the ponytail holder and gave a deep growl. Every vibration of the sound was animalistic. There was no pretty towheaded girlfriend in bed with Justin anymore. There was only a canine, a sultry bitch in heat.

"That's it," Justin said, obviously surprised. He kept up the motion, his cock working steadily between my legs, but now he unfastened the leash and doubled it in his hand. "That's the girl," he continued, urging me on.

My next attempt was more doglike, an urgent, insistent barking sound. Justin rewarded me by fucking me harder and faster, his fingers plucking a melody out on my clit, taking me higher. And as I grew closer to climax, the barking continued. I couldn't believe it was me making these noises. But maybe it wasn't me. Maybe it was the pet that I'd become. As I got louder, Justin took on his proper role as my owner.

"Keep it down, girl," he said, a definite retraction of what he'd asked me for before. "The neighbors will complain. They'll think we actually have a pet in here. It might actually get to the landlord."

That only made me bark louder. I wanted to come. I wanted him to slam into me with everything he had.

"Bad doggy," he scowled, bringing the doubled-up leash against my ass. I whimpered at the punishing blow. "Bad doggy," he said again, smacking the other haunch with the leash. He worked me seriously with the belt, striping my hide over and over. I could picture the instant berry-red welts against my pale skin, and I raised up to meet each blow. Discipline is the magic that holds me together. "You listen to your owner. You be a good girl."

But I wouldn't. I growled and yipped. I pretended there

was a full yellow moon outside, and I threw back my head and howled. Other dogs in the neighborhood answered my wails and soon there was a cacophony of canine noises filling the air.

"We're going to have to have a few solid lessons in obedience training," Justin scolded me as he dropped the leash and gripped my hips. "A lot of long hours with your head on the floor at my feet, doing exactly what I say. You're going to have to learn to lie down. To sit. To stay. You're going to have to learn how to be a good puppy for me. Now, behave—"

But no matter how serious his tone of voice, I wouldn't behave as he demanded. I continued to bark, my voice rising, and Justin pulled away from the bed, a frown marring his handsome features. While I watched, he reached for the newspaper on the nightstand and spread the paper out on the floor. Then he glared at me.

"Down—," he said.

I didn't move. He let the belt land on my ass several times in a row in the hardest strokes I'd ever felt. Then he let up and gave me a second chance.

"Down," he said again. "Now."

Quickly, I started to move off the bed.

"Like a dog," he hissed through gritted teeth. So, like a dog, I moved on all fours off the bed to the paper-covered floor. "This is your bed tonight."

I gazed up at him, concerned, but he wouldn't say another word. Quietly, heart racing, I curled myself up at his feet. Justin gazed down at me, then nodded to himself and retreated to our bed. I heard the mattress moving as he jacked off, but he didn't ask me to join him. My eyes on the window, I watched the moonlight. My pussy throbbed, but I didn't touch myself. I lay there, breathing softly, until I fell asleep.

In the morning, I was surprised to find myself on the spread-out newsprint, surprised to see Justin with his leash in hand, standing at my side. I started to rise, and he put one hand on my shoulder, pushing me back down. With a firm gesture, he locked the leash onto my collar, then tugged me upright.

"Obedience school begins now," he said.

My lips parted, but he shook his head.

"You'll be punished," he assured me, "for each infraction. Behave yourself, little doggy, if you know what's good for you."

I followed after him on hands and knees as he led me from our bedroom down the hall until we reached the French doors leading to our plush backyard. "You use the dirt out here when you need to go," he said, showing me my spot, "and when you're finished, you wait for me here." He pointed to a rattan mat he'd set out on the wood porch.

His eyes were on me, staring hard, and I realized suddenly that he was actually waiting for me to pee in the backyard. Most bizarre situation ever. I wouldn't do it. But he was waiting, and I had to go. I had to. What kept me from standing up and walking down the hall like a grown-up woman to our bathroom? I don't know. The look in his eyes. Maybe. The fact that I'd confessed to him this very fantasy the night before. Probably. While Justin watched, I scampered off the porch to a square of dirt and squatted, pissing on the dark earth while he nodded his approval. When I came back to his side, he scratched the back of my head and led me back into our house.

I thought he would fuck me. I thought he would give in to the game playing and just fuck me, rocket inside me and let me transform back into myself. But he was serious about his obedience training, and with the leash still attached to my collar, he led me back to our room and positioned me in front of our mirrors.

"Down," he said, and I humbly fell at his feet. "Now, sit,"

he commanded, and I easily obeyed. "Good girl," he said, "now go and fetch my slippers."

I crawled to the closet and nudged the door open, then reached for his leather bedroom slippers with my hand.

"With your mouth—" Justin demanded. I glanced over my shoulder at him, and saw that he wasn't kidding. I shook my head, and he was on me in an instant. "You obey me when I give you an order," he said, and the leather leash was unbuckled from my collar, and once again I found myself on the receiving end of the ferociously stinging blows. I bent down, cowering, as the leash found my bare ass again and again, and I realized just how much I desired the pain he rained down on me.

"Again," he said. "We try again." But I wouldn't put my mouth on those shoes, so he hauled me back in place for a second brutal encounter with the flailing leather strip of that leash. My ass was on fire. My thighs burning up. Each stripe of the belt made me more his obedient pet and less his girlfriend.

"Behave—" he hissed, and as something seemed to tear inside me, I lowered my head and took one slipper and then the other into my mouth, making two trips to bring my Master his shoes.

The quality of my surrender made Justin harder than steel. He lifted me onto the bed and took me again, on all fours, exactly as I deserved to be fucked. My pussy was dripping wet; I was as turned on as I'd ever been in my life. Justin's cock drove inside of me with ease, and I saw myself as exactly who I was—who I'd always wanted to be. His pet. His puppy dog. Subservient to my Master.

I looked into the mirror again and saw Justin reaching his limits. He lowered his head as the climax built within him, and he continued to fuck me just as hard as I needed it. Right at his peak, he touched my clit, just touched it, and I came with him, the explosions ricocheting back and forth between us.

He fell onto the bed and I curled up next to him, licking his lips with my tongue, kissing his face all over. I was still hungry, worked up, and I moved down his body until my mouth was poised over his cock. I started slowly, licking the tip, then moving in a line all the way down to lick my sticky juices off of it. Nuzzling my face against him, I lapped at his slippery pole. Then I took him into my mouth and felt his rod grow quickly hard again. I didn't speak, didn't make any noise at all. I was still his pet, but now I was his humble, subservient pet, and I worked as hard as I could to let him know how pleased I was.

He knew.

"Good doggy," Justin grinned as I sucked him. He petted my long hair as my mouth took him in. "Oh, Celia, you know you can be such a good fucking doggy when you try."

EVER ON EDGE

Debra Hyde

Nina managed to get to the phone at the third ring. She steadfastly refused to screen her calls, a decision that forever pitted her against the answering machine in a race to pick up before the fourth ring engaged it, but she had good reason for her compulsion.

"Hello?" She knew she sounded harried, rushed.

"Put your hand up your blouse."

Instantly, her hand went into motion, creeping up her blouse—but then, Nina knew the voice that commanded her.

"Grasp your breast," the voice commanded.

Her hand was swiftly upon her breast in synch with the command. "I have," she answered. She smiled wanly. *Phone domination with your husband,* she thought, *is a lot like taking driving lessons from your father. He tells you what to do just as your foot reaches for the brakes.*

"Now take your nipple and pinch it."

"Yes." Her voice grew breathy. The authority in his voice amazed her.

"Pull on it. More. Stretch it out."

Nina's idle thoughts fell by the wayside as the sensations of teasing herself overtook her and arousal rose as she complied with her husband's order. For his part, Steven didn't release Nina from her own grip until she moaned loudly, confirming that she had given sway to him.

"You can let go now," he instructed, pleased with the outcome. Instantly, his initial take-no-prisoners voice changed for a chipper, "Good afternoon!"

"Well, hello to you too!" Nina countered in pleasant sarcasm.

Steven's hearty peal of laughter told her that he appreciated her comeback. She loved to make him laugh and she appreciated the place that her sense of humor had in their relationship. Still, Nina needed to know that she hadn't violated any Master/slave boundary.

"I say that only for comic relief, Sir. I hope you approve."

"Indeed I do," Steven reassured her. "But on another matter, have you secured tickets for the play this Friday?"

Nina hadn't and she froze, speechless. Within seconds of posing the question, Steven laughed quietly but knowingly. Indeed, he knew her well. When Nina succeeded in doing his bidding, she would respond with instant, breathless enthusiasm. When she hadn't, she would say nothing. And silence was golden.

"Oh my, how dreadfully inattentive of you," Steven mocked.

Nina blushed—she always did—and she knew that was why Steven teased her. But it was all in erotic fun, if for no other reason than that she was so easy to move to both embarrassment and wetness. And she liked it as well; she liked that feeling of becoming small, of shrinking into that shy inner corner somewhere within herself.

"Well, I'll have to keep in mind what a procrastinator you are, my darling," Steven continued. "Call for the tickets now. I'll see you Friday afternoon. Be sure you're dressed to code when you meet me at the airport. Oh, and make it a tight sweater."

"Yes, Sir," she answered dutifully. She heard Steven hang up and when the dial tone sounded, she reached for the phone book and looked for the ticket office's number.

Friday was gray with warm drizzle, El Niño influenced if not induced. As Nina drove to the airport, the wipers groaned and scraped against the windshield, but the fine spray of drizzle was just strong enough that going without the wipers was impossible. The sound annoyed her but other than her worn patience, the drive to the airport was routine enough. Good thing that meeting Steven at the airport was always tinged with the excitement of reunion, no matter how routine the drive itself had become.

Nina had waited for all of ten minutes when Steven's plane wheeled into place and people began to disembark. It had become something of a private ritual for her to intently watch for him and soon enough, she caught that first glimpse.

She fluttered with excitement as Steven strolled toward her, overcoat in one hand, computer case in the other. He lowered the latter to the floor to take her into his arms and kiss her. Nina melted into his embrace, marveling at how their bodies still melded perfectly together after all these years. Neither their intimate fit nor her appreciation of it had diminished over time.

Steven's kiss was strong and insistent, and Nina knew he wanted her. "A week on the road does that to a man," he'd once joked with her, "so perhaps you'd better get use to being seized at the airport. The search we'll save for later."

The mundane parts of their reunion followed—the lemming-like journey to the baggage carousel, retrieving Steven's one and only suitcase, heading for the parking lot. After they reached the car and Steven stowed his belongings in the trunk, he took Nina by the arm, led her around to the passenger side, and took her again in an even lustier kiss and embrace.

Nina responded, accepting his desire, but at the same time, her posture stiffened, telling him that such a public display of affection scared her. Rather than making him wary, her shyness energized him and he pressed into her, pinning her against the car. The healthy erection stowed in his pants pressed between her legs, an undeniable reminder of his eagerness.

"Be thankful it's so busy here," he whispered to her, nibbling her ear and caressing her hair, "or I'd have you take that out and stroke it right here." He pressed his cock into her, leaving no question as to what "that" might be.

Nina whimpered.

In response, Steven reached for her breast, cupped it, and caressed it.

"A quick feel, that's all I want." He felt her nipple harden at his touch, at his words, and he smiled. He broke away from her and went around to the driver's side of the car.

Nina, however, was left panting and wanting.

Steven kept her that way while they traveled home. Adeptly, he crept his hand up her leg, dragging her floral print skirt up her thigh as he found his way to her clit. His touch was electrifying and Nina found her body more than ready, given the abstinence order he'd imposed on her earlier in the week. A few seconds of deep massaging had Nina swooning toward orgasm. Swiftly, Steven removed his hand and thwarted her.

"Can't have that," he teased, patting her thigh before returning his hand to the steering wheel. He was gleefully patronizing.

Nina looked down at her lap. Her disheveled skirt seemed

to symbolize what she had almost had, but Steven paid no attention to her condition until a few minutes had passed and her
arousal abated. Then, he noticed her sweater, tightly buttoned
down its center.

"That's a nice sweater you have on," he commented casually.

"Thank you, Sir." Nina knew Steven well enough to guess
where this was going.

"Unbutton it. Show me your tits."

No matter how practiced Nina was with this little ritual,
Steven's order always shocked her enough to make her fumble
through the unbuttoning. As she complied, she blushed and
smiled, the blush revealing mild humiliation, the smile reflecting
her lust for it. Undoing the sweater seemed to take an eternity,
but in mere moments of real time she had opened it and revealed
her small, dainty, ever-braless breasts.

"Lovely," he said. "You may let go of your top."

A nondescript SUV sped by on their right. Its occupant looked
down toward their car. Nina made eye contact as she let go of
her sweater and startled.

"May I button?" she asked, flustered.

Steven shot her a sideways you've-got-to-be-kidding glance.
Then he softened and smiled. "You'll be fine," he said tenderly.

Home, however, was a different matter. Steven cast aside his
overcoat and baggage, plopped down in his favorite easy chair,
and pointed to the floor before his feet. On that very spot, Nina
fell to her knees like a well-trained dog.

Steven eased back into the chair.

"Come closer. Unzip me. Take out my cock and suck it."

Nina freed his flaccid member and brought it into her mouth,
encompassing it with her lips. Gently, she set to work. Licking
and tonguing its shaft, its head, she felt it grow to life in her

mouth and blossom, erect and sturdy. She felt it throb, once, twice, and she heard Steven groan.

Without warning, he gripped the back of her head and forced her down fully on his cock. Nina struggled to take all of him but, realizing that she couldn't, she balked. No matter how practiced she had tried to become, her gag reflex remained forever too sensitive. But Steven loved this weakness in her and held her in place until she calmed.

"Now take a little more," he urged her as he less-than-inched his cock deeper. Nina gagged, struggled to breathe around it. She huffed like a winded racehorse. He held her there, then added yet a little more length to her struggle. This time, she began to retch.

"Just a moment longer," he said, comforting her even as he insisted she stay put. "You're doing fine."

Steven drew himself back and then pushed in deeply; Nina nearly retched again and she whimpered, the only kind of begging she could manage while orally impaled. Steven laughed, enjoying her predicament.

But he did appreciate the fact that she'd suffered enough. For Steven, deep-throating was a power play, not a road to orgasm. He preferred to fuck her mouth in a more shallow fashion, allowing Nina to concentrate on that sweet spot just below the head of his dick. He got off best when all the pleasure was concentrated at the end of his cock, not when it was lodged in the back of her throat.

As she pleasured him, Steven raised Nina's skirt and gathered it around her waist. The round globes of her ass jutted out as she knelt and sucked. Steven reached over her back and caressed her ass. Marveling at how soft and pliant she felt, he remembered the feel of her tight asshole as he fucked it, and his cock pulsed massively enough in her mouth to make her groan.

Ah, yes, her ass was something.

He raised his hand and planted two swift blows on her, one to each cheek. Nina squirmed but stayed attentive to her cocksucking. Ah, he loved how she squirmed. So the spanking continued, one smack after another landing cheek to cheek. Steven kept his pace slow and steady, knowing Nina would experience a warm glow, knowing it would lull her into a comfortable, even complacent arousal. Nina, her mouth still attentive, felt his focus zero in on her. Her own awareness had narrowed to the cock in her mouth and the hand on her ass, as if she existed for nothing else. They held her captive.

Steven sensed Nina shrinking into herself. Now was the time to push, to test. He sent a flurry of fast, powerful slaps across Nina's ass. The spanking became relentless and Nina no long squirmed. She writhed. She cried out from around his cock, tormented instead of pleasured, tested instead of lulled. And when she couldn't take it anymore, she pulled herself off of her husband's shaft and screamed.

Steven grabbed the back of her head, forced her back onto his cock, and spanked her even harder, chastising her with every blow.

"Did I tell you to take your mouth off my cock? Did I?"

Between the fierce spanking and being held in place, Nina could only sob despairingly, her cries leaking out from around Steven's hard cock.

Once he had her at that point, Steven reached down along the cushion of the chair and pulled some clover clamps out of hiding. "Up," he commanded Nina, releasing her from his cock.

Nina knelt upright and looked at Steven through dazed eyes—but not too dazed to miss the clamps. "Oh, please no," she whimpered.

"Remove your sweater," Steven ordered.

Nina tossed it to the floor. Her breasts, petite globes far firmer than her ass, stood ready, nipples erect.

Steven approached her with the clover clamps. Nina couldn't watch and closed her eyes tightly. Yet she knew Steven's every move: how he'd pinched one nipple between his fingers, how the cruel clamp would close around it, how it would sting and burn, and how he'd repeat the process with the other nipple. Nina sucked in her breath as a tight pinch seized each nipple. Then she relaxed her breathing, as if a Lamaze-like technique would help her through the pain.

But Steven was not content to let her merely grow used to the pain, such as it was. He took hold of the clamps' chain and pulled. Nina groaned miserably, for the clamps did more than stretch her nipples. Literally, they pinched harder and deeper. Steven twisted the chain to the left, then right. Nina shuddered and cried out. "Oh, please!" was all she could beg.

Yet Nina flushed wet with arousal even as she whimpered. No matter what struggle Steven foisted on her, surrendering to his will primed her for fucking.

And Steven wanted her surrender. He reached for her skirt, unbuttoned it, and let it fall away. He reached between her legs and assessed her readiness.

"You're wet, slut. Know that?" he cajoled.

"Yes, Sir." Nina's whisper was breathy, made distant by desire.

"I wonder what would happen if I do this," Steven speculated. He slipped a finger between her slick lips and buried it inside her. He laid his thumb across her clit and pressed. Nina melted, almost instantly orgasmic. Steven circled his thumb around her clit, strummed it back and forth, and felt her clit harden in his hand.

"Ah, your cunt wants to come, doesn't it?" he mused.

Nina groaned plaintively. Lust clouded her.

"Do it, slut. Come for me."

There it was—*slut*, that magic word! Her cunt convulsed when Steven said it. Feeling her reaction, Steven continued. "Slut," he repeated. "Come for me, slut, so I can fuck you."

That did it. The thought of getting fucked pushed Nina over the edge. She came, crying out in a noisy, prolonged throbbing and thrashing. Once spent, she collapsed into Steven's arms.

He eased her onto her back, splayed her legs apart and lay himself over her. In one sure push, he entered her, then rode her hard and fast. Although Nina roused once more to orgasm, he focused largely on himself. He raised himself up on his hands and looked down at her clamped tits and their sorely compromised nipples. He brushed his hand across them. Nina squirmed and moaned, and the sight of her struggle forced him very close to coming. He grabbed the clamps' chain and pulled on them one last time.

Nina's scream rose up to meet the sound of blood rushing in Steven's ears just as his orgasm hit. He exploded and rode wave upon wave of release as his lover writhed beneath him. Her pain, his pleasure merged into one moment, a moment so complete in its peak and resolution that when Steven collapsed onto Nina, she'd forgotten all about the clamps, her awareness consumed by the incredible fucking that had just concluded.

In time, they collected their wits. Steven removed the clamps—Nina cried out one last time as he did—and they readied for their evening out. Jovially, they jockeyed for the shower, two lovers familiar with each other's ways and in love with that familiarity. Even if that familiarity included a second spanking to refresh Nina's skin. Even if it included a patch of fine sandpaper inside her panties, one for each cheek.

"Ouch!" she mock-complained when she first sat down in the car.

"That's just how I like you," he teased with a gleeful glint in his eyes. "Always on the edge of your seat."

Nina smiled broadly. She couldn't help it. Because that's just how she liked things, too.

FIVE BUCKS
A SWAT

Christopher Pierce

There was something different in the air that night, something that said, *Tonight is going to be special.* Tony hadn't said anything out of the ordinary as we dressed to go out, but as the bottom in a dominant/submissive relationship, I was used to being told only what I absolutely needed to know. There'd been plenty of surprises in the six months Tony and I had been seeing each other.

But tonight was special.

Tony had told me to wear what he called my "jailhouse shorts," a pair of too-tight workout briefs that were black-and-white-striped. They clearly showed the twin globes of hard flesh that made up my bubble butt. Tony loved my butt, describing it as "perfect" on more than one occasion.

He had many uses for my ass—burying his face in it, fucking it with dildos or his fingers, as well as his favorite: spanking it. I loved it when Tony spanked me, and he loved doing it—I think it was our favorite thing to do, aside from him fucking the shit out of me.

I finished dressing myself with a white tank top that showed off my lean chest and flat stomach. Tony came up behind me and encircled my slender neck with a leather collar that was studded with short, blunt spikes. It was a ceremonial collar—a collar for show, so we were probably going to be around other people. He came around to admire his boy toy, and I saw that he was dressed in a plain T-shirt, jeans, boots, and leather jacket. He never liked to draw attention to himself when he had me around—I was what he wanted people to look at. He liked to show me off whenever the opportunity presented itself.

After securing the collar around my neck with a small padlock, he told me to put on my military boots. I did what he said, then followed him out of his condo to where his new truck was parked. When we got in, Tony tied a blindfold over my eyes and had me adjust my seat way back so I wouldn't be visible to other drivers.

And so I wouldn't have any idea where we were going.

Then we were off.

In my disoriented condition I couldn't tell where he was taking us to. We drove for about twenty minutes, but that didn't tell me anything—we could've been anywhere in the city.

I felt him slow the truck down and then parallel park. He got out and came around to my side. Opening my door, he helped me out of the truck but didn't take the blindfold off.

"Do you trust me?" he asked.

"Yes, Sir," I said, even though I was a little scared. Scared, but also excited.

"Everything will be okay," he said.

"I believe you, Sir," I said.

"Come on," Tony said, putting his hands on my shoulders. As he led me away from the truck, I heard him close the door and activate the vehicle's alarm. He guided me along the street and then down into a driveway. I heard the muffled sounds of music and lots of voices. My anticipation increased at the noises.

He led me up some stairs and through a door.

Now the sounds were joined by odors—beer, smoke, and lots of men. I heard some jeers and laughter as I was guided through what must have been a large crowd.

An amplified voice rang out, drowning out the other sounds.

"Here we go, guys," it said, "Give it up for Master Tony Gardner, who has graciously provided us with the first subject for tonight's event!"

Subject? Event? What's going on here? I thought.

But there was no time to question because I was forced up a short flight of stairs onto what must have been a stage where the voice of the master of ceremonies was much louder.

"What's happening?" I whispered.

"Trust me," Tony said in my ear, and then other hands took me. I was bent over something wooden, probably a table, my arms stretched out and bound with leather shackles. I struggled, but the shackles had been secured to something solid, probably the wall. My legs were spread wide and my ankles shackled to what must have been the legs of the table. Last but not least, my shorts were yanked down, my naked butt exposed to the room and my cock and balls hanging free at the edge of the table.

The crowd of men whooped and hollered at the sight of my ass, and I blushed with excitement and embarrassment even though no one could see my face.

"Step right up, men!" the emcee said. "Be the first to lay your hands on this beautiful butt!"

What?!? I thought.

"What's this boy's name, Master Tony?"

"He answers to the name of Spanky," I heard Tony say, raising a roar of laughter from the crowd.

"Five bucks a swat, guys, five bucks a swat!" the emcee continued. "And it's for a wonderful cause—the Gay Center's Youth Task Force, providing food and shelter to homeless gay kids. Who's going to be first to spank this ass for charity?"

Goose bumps rose on every inch of my body as I tried to comprehend what I'd just heard. Spanked for charity? This was incredible, and undeniably hot—but it didn't matter what I thought, I realized—I was in no position to object!

The emcee's voice boomed through the air.

"You, sir," he was saying, "come on up here! You'll be the first to spank Spanky's ass tonight. How much are you donating to our worthy cause?"

"Thirty dollars," a new voice said. "I'd do more but it's all I have on me."

"Fantastic! Thirty dollars—that's six swats on this magnificent ass!"

The man's hand felt good on my buttcheek as he rubbed it a little, and I felt my cock getting hard in anticipation. This was all so incredible—was it a dream?

Any questions about this experience's reality were banished a second later when the first swat hit my left asscheek with a loud smacking sound. It hurt like hell, but it made my dick flex at the same time. The second and third swats were even harder, and the crowd rumbled its approval as the remaining blows fell.

"Well done, sir!" the emcee boomed. "Just the warm-up we needed! Who's next?"

I wondered where Tony was—I was disoriented and still couldn't see a thing. I resisted the urge to be scared—Tony had asked me to trust him and I had agreed.

"You there! With all the tattoos—how much are you going to give to help those kids?"

"Fifty bucks!" a deep voice answered.

"Come on up. Ten swats, gentlemen, ten swats on this choice piece of boymeat butt!"

The men cheered in excitement.

Tattoo man alternated with his spanking, first one cheek, then the other. But all his swats were hard. The whole time the emcee spoke into his microphone, a running commentary that pounded in my ears.

"We've got some good color coming out there, guys, look at Spanky's cheeks turning nice and pink!"

Smack! on my left cheek. "Nine!"

Smack! on my right cheek. "Ten!"

"And that's ten swats! Thank you, sir, for donating to our worthy cause!"

"I'm next!" a voice bellowed from the crowd.

"Yes, you with the motorcycle cap, get on up here!"

I heard the stairs creak as my latest tormentor walked up to the stage. *He must be a big guy,* I thought with a hint of panic. He's probably got a hell of a swat. I found myself tensing up, my knees locking and my buttocks clenching. I knew it was a stupid thing to do—I'd learned from past experience that it doesn't help and can sometimes make it worse to get tense when you're being spanked. But I couldn't help it, I was scared.

"How many swats are you buying, sir?" the emcee asked.

"Only have money for three," the loud voice said, "so I'm gonna make 'em count."

The motorcycle cap man's first swat was like a thunderbolt, his hand connecting with my ass so hard that I cried out in pain. He didn't do one cheek at a time like the other guys had; he aimed right for my butt crack and got both at the same time. He must've had a really big hand. Before I could catch my breath the second swat came, exploding against me with enough force to bring tears to my eyes and force another yelp of agony out of me.

The assembled men groaned sympathetically—my ass must've been bright red by then. I was ready for motorcycle cap man's third swat, but it didn't make it any less painful. I bit back a third scream, not wanting to hear it myself, maybe afraid to hear it myself.

The crowd roared in approval.

"Three unforgettable swats!" the emcee said, "Thank you for your fifteen dollars, sir, it's going to help a lot of people."

No more, I thought, *please no more.* But somehow, through all of this, my cock had stayed hard. Maybe I didn't want this to end as much as I thought I did.

"All right, gentlemen, we're ready for another volunteer— yes, sir, you'd like to go next? Is that a one-hundred-dollar bill in your hand?"

I tried not to freak out—twenty swats—how could I take that? How could I take any of this? It was more intense than anything I'd experienced before. Think of Tony, I told myself. Think of his warm, caring eyes; think of his low, soothing voice; think of how good it feels when he puts his hands on me....

But instead of my lover's reassuring touch what I felt next was a hard smack on my butt from the big spender. It was painful, but at least not as bad as the beating I'd gotten from motorcycle cap man. I endured the pain as best I could, gritting my teeth as sweat began to drip down my face. I was starting to get sore from being bound in one place for so long, but there was nothing I could do—no one could have heard me yell for help over the noise of the crowd, and no one would help me if I did.

The big spender had his own style of spanking. The first five swats were hard and painful, but the next five were soft and gentle, more pats than swats. My punished flesh was grateful for even a short break from the pain, but the third five were once again painful strikes. My ass must've been bright cherry red by then, and it felt like raw hamburger. I hardly felt the final, softer five; it almost felt like my butt was going numb.

After the big spender was done I started to lose track of time. The emcee kept talking and the swats kept coming, but I was lost in a hazy cloud of pain, fear, fatigue, and sexual desire.

Just as I felt like I couldn't take any more, the emcee's voice penetrated my daze.

"Okay, I think Spanky's had enough for one night. We've raised almost $700; let's give him a hand, come on, men, give it up for the boy!" Loud applause and cheers followed. "Let's have just one more donation. Who will it be, guys, who'll be the last man to spank this boy tonight?"

There was a short pause—for the first time that night, it seemed like something had happened that made the emcee speechless.

Then: "Master Tony? You want to pay to spank your own boy?"

"It's worth paying for," I heard Tony say.

My heart leapt at his voice. I didn't realize how much I'd missed him—I'd almost forgotten he was there, I'd felt so isolated, so alone in my private hell of pain. Then his voice was in my ear.

"Everything's going to be okay," he whispered.

"I believe you, Sir," I said, echoing my earlier statement.

"Twenty-five dollars from Master Tony!" the emcee said. "Watch the last five swats for Spanky!"

Tony rested one hand on the small of my back, the other on my flaming ass. Then he raised his hand.

I closed my eyes behind the blindfold.

Smack!

"One!" roared the emcee

The pain was like an explosion in my buttcheek.

Smack!

"Two!" the crowd joined the emcee in the count.

But what was happening?

Tony was reaching between my legs and taking my still rock-hard cock in his hand!

Smack!

"Three!"

He was jerking me off with one hand and spanking me with the other! The pain in my ass and the pleasure in my crotch mixed, hurting and confusing me, but taking me so high I felt like I like I was having an out-of-body experience.

Smack!

"Four!"

I couldn't take much more of this—I was on total sensory overload. My butt was blazing with a fire whose intensity was matched only by the inferno of ecstasy between my legs.

Smack!

"Five!"

As Tony's last swat hit I came, squirting my sperm onto the floor beneath the table where I was bound. The crowd went wild, cheering and clapping like they'd just seen the winning touchdown at a football game. At the same instant something broke inside me. The anticipation, fear, pain, and pleasure of the last few hours came to a boiling point—and I started crying. Tears squeezed out from beneath my tightly closed eyelids and dripped down my face.

I hardly felt it when my wrists were released from the restraints that held me to the table. My ankles were freed next, and I almost stumbled to the floor of the stage I was so exhausted and disoriented. The blindfold was removed, and I squinted at the bright lights that were hitting the stage. Someone pulled my shorts back up, the fabric somehow stinging and soothing

my butt at the same time. I dimly recognized the place as one of
the city's leather bars, and I saw the crowd of men in their best
jeans and leather.

But mostly, I saw Tony.

He was grinning at me.

"You did good," he said.

"Thank you, Sir," I said, and stumbled again.

Tony caught me before I fell and bent over, hoisting me
gently up and over his shoulder. He adjusted me for maximum
comfort and secured my legs in place with one arm. He carried
me down the stairs to the cheering of the crowd. I was too tired
to do anything but hang limply over Tony's shoulder, just happy
that it was all over and that I was safe in his arms. As he carried
me out of the bar I heard the emcee start the whole thing over
again.

"Okay, guys, the next spanking boy is being provided by
Master Richard...."

The quiet and the fresh air of the street were most welcome.
Tony carried me over his shoulder for the whole walk back to
his truck. When he set me down next to the parked vehicle, I
grinned back at him.

"Five bucks a swat, huh?" I said.

"You're worth much more," Tony said, "but I figured it was
all they could afford."

EVERYTHING THAT YOU WANT

C. D. Formetta
Translated by Maxim Jakubowski

If you are born a slave, you will also die a slave.

Don't listen to anyone who says otherwise, and don't believe those who say they spend their time ordering others around, but who in private prefer to be dominated. They are lying to you.

Slavery is not a choice, and neither is it a lifestyle. Or a set of clothes you only wear a few hours every day. Slavery is both a sentence and a virtue. It's a punishment one must be proud to earn. It is the pain of brutal intercourse that draws you to pleasure. It's the voice of your Master ordering you to do something and the mark of his fingertips searching between your legs until it hurts. But pain is also a sweeter form of pleasure.

I was born a slave thirty-five years ago. My parents shaped my will into the virtues of obedience. They always chose for me, first my friends, then university, and of course the young men I was allowed to go out with; then the husband I wed. I did everything according to their will, without ever complaining. I graduated in architecture, frequented the best families, only went out with serious and respectable young men, and finally I married Alberto.

I married him and almost immediately betrayed him.

You might say that's a contradiction in terms, an awful form of rebellion, but it defined me as a slave. Or maybe not.

But it was no rebellion, because Alberto is not my Master, and never was.

Alberto doesn't really know who I am. He looks at me and only sees his adorable wife, a woman to be looked after, treated with respect.

I am aware I am not worthy of his respect.

I forget the roast in the oven, only remember to take it out when it's badly burned and I say nothing to him about it. I drive the car against a lamppost, and he stays calm. He forgives me.

At least once I would like Alberto to slap me. Just once would I like to receive the punishment I deserve. If Alberto had somehow been my Master, he would already have dragged me into the room and ripped my nightdress off my back, thrown it to the ground and left me there, naked and humiliated before his eyes. He would beat me just because he felt like doing so, pinch my nipples until the pain roared.

Had Alberto somehow become my Master, I would have been his faithful slave, forever. But Alberto doesn't have the character, or the necessary inner strength to impose himself on and dominate me. Alberto always takes a shower before he makes love because he is afraid his smell will bother me, and he sleeps wearing a cotton vest because he has allergies, suffers from dermatitis and scratches himself all night.

Alberto is a discreet and well-educated husband, but he is not my true Master.

My Master is another.

* * *

I met Franco two years back, on the occasion of a work dinner.

We were introduced and quickly discovered how much we had in common: his work as an architect, his passion for French cinema, a fond affection for jazz. Most of all we were brought together by the discovery of these similarities. We completed each other.

He was a dominant; that was obvious at first glance, just watching the way he moved and spoke. His gestures were precise and secure, he never hesitated or stumbled. His words did not make demands, they just affirmed the certitude of his will. And his answers obviously precluded any comeback.

Franco was born to command, and I was consumed inside by the will to obey him. Together we formed a perfect combination.

We chatted all evening about everything and nothing, our conversation full of banalities, clichés, maybe so as not to provide any suspicion to the other guests.

Following the dinner, Franco offered to walk me back home, and no one else objected. I had drunk; not too much, but I pretended I had, so that his offer did not sound unusual. It was the first of many times I would say yes to Franco.

We had almost reached my house, when Franco changed his mind.

"Come with me," he said.

"Yes," I replied.

That night, Franco became my Master.

Franco's house was big and luxurious. It was the house of a well-to-do man who had no problems showing off how rich he was. It was built on two levels, and you entered it through a lounge, and the bedroom could only be reached through a small flight of stairs.

"Go up," he ordered. "I want to see how you move."

I obeyed. I was wearing a black evening dress which clung tightly to my hips, and left much of my legs uncovered. As I slowly walked up the narrow stairs I knew that his eyes were examining my body. He kept on watching me as I stood in his room, and I felt short of breath.

"You slip into a total stranger's bedroom, and you say nothing?" he asked me. "I could be a madman, a maniac. I could do anything to you, even kill you. You wouldn't be able to escape, there's nowhere here to hide yourself."

I didn't know what to think. I was frightened and he was in charge.

"Are you afraid of me?"

"Yes," I said. And his hand slid between my legs.

"Are you afraid of me?" Franco repeated, while his finger slipped into my cunt and explored my insides like a hook drilling through bait. "Are you afraid of me?"

"Yes," I moaned. Then Franco pulled his hand away and caressed my cheeks. His fingers were still wet from me.

"Liar."

He made me stretch out on the bed and slowly undressed me. He enjoyed witnessing my lack of resistance, seeing that I would allow him to do whatever he wished to me.

"Franco...," I hesitantly said. But he put his hand against my mouth.

"Stay quiet," he said. "I don't want you to say my name."

He then unbuttoned his shirt, slipped out of his trousers and stood there, by the bed, facing me naked.

"Look at me."

And I looked. The Master was short and thin, with his cock out of all proportion with the rest of his body. His arms were covered by short, curly black hair, all the way down from his shoulders. I didn't find his body pleasant. However I couldn't take my eyes off him.

Now, the Master wanted to see me better.

"Open your legs."

Once again I was obedient and yielded.

"Open, I said!"

The Master took hold of my ankles and forcefully pushed my legs wide apart, lowered his eyes, and began examining me in full detail.

"You're tight," he said. "Hasn't your husband yet used you thoroughly?"

I didn't quite understand what he was on about until the moment he violently slammed himself into me.

"Your husband doesn't know how to fuck you, I see."

No, I wanted to scream. My husband doesn't know what to do with me, he doesn't understand that I have no need for kisses, or embraces. Not even a caress is necessary. Only the hands of my Master forcing my legs wide, and his cock traveling so deep inside me, ripping me open like a piece of meat, sundering my life apart.

One part of my life was with Alberto and his romantic and repetitive attentions. My other life was fully devoted to my Master. From today onward, with him, I would travel this new road.

That evening, the Master allowed me to leave. But had he asked me to stay there, in his bed, all night long, I would have accepted, as I would have also agreed to return to him the following day, and again the day after. Every time he desired me, I would grant his desire.

Many believe that slavery is violence, torture, a simple affair of whips and chains, but that's not the way it is. *Real* slavery is so much more complicated.

Slavery is most of all a mental attitude. It means being aware of one's own limits and understanding that if you are not strong enough to be in charge, you should be strong enough to accept the authority of someone who is.

My Master has no need to jail me, to gag me or have me wear a hood of black latex. These are theatrical props, accessories for bourgeois couples seeking a mildly transgressive evening.

Slavery is being a thing, just an object for another's pleasure with no questions asked, unconditionally.

The Master calls me to join him, and I run to him. The Master demands I not touch him, that I do not say his name, and I stay spread-eagled on the bed without moving, utterly silent, while he is free to do anything he wishes.

When we are together, the Master knows I am no longer a person. In those moments, I am just a body, of which he will dispose however he will.

I go along with all his demands.

One night, my Master insisted on massaging my back. He had done so on other occasions, and I knew what he wanted of me. I turned onto my stomach and allowed him to proceed. I felt very tender. He sprayed some perfumed oil over my body and began to stroke me with slow and light movements, first my back, then my shoulders, and finally my legs. I could feel his fingers moving towards my pubis, barely grazing it then moving away again. Nothing else happened that night. It entertained him to excite me this way, bringing me close to pleasure and then denying it. It made him feel even more strong and powerful. And this did not make me angry, neither did I return home straight afterward and ask my husband to make love to me so as to calm my fever down, or take a cold bath or shower that would have helped me think less of him, to desire him less. I knew that I must remain this way, hot and quivering, until the time came for our next encounter. This is what the Master expected of me, and I would never deceive him. Ever.

That night, my Master continued to touch me until my body could not bear it anymore and my patience was strung out like a bow, and he masturbated in my presence while I was required to watch, and I envied him this moment of release because he was free to do what he wanted. Only he had the power to give and take.

There were other times. And on every occasion, the Master made the same mistake.

It's not that I really envied him, there was no reason to. He gave me everything that I wanted, everything that I ever needed. He provided me with rules, orders, tasks to complete before his return. I kept my mind occupied and distant from my simpering conjugal life, outwardly perfect and harmonic, but in truth so dull and lifeless. Motionless on the bed, with my Master taking care of me, I was happy. I finally had everything I wanted, everything I had ever dreamed of.

I loved him. I loved my Master with blind and absolute devotion. I loved him so much it became impossible not to express it in my emotions.

"You are everything I want," I said to him....

I felt him stiffen. Unexpectedly, the Master moved his hands away from me and became distant. He looked at me with a new expression on his face, his eyes were far away. He was angry.

"Who said you could even *want something?*" he shouted. "You do not have my permission to desire me or any one else. You no longer have desires, you no longer have any will."

I had disappointed him. I had understood nothing.

I understood that soon the Master would get rid of me.

Once again, I find myself traveling down a one-way road, living a one-way life. The Master no longer summons me, and I do not attempt to make contact with him. I know that should I do so I would anger him even more. I had no news from him for a long, unending period, but I allowed the weeks, the months to go by, hoping that somehow it would soothe the pain slightly.

I have withstood the temptation to take other lovers or new masters. I finally accepted Alberto's proposal to go out on a Saturday to do the shopping together, like so many of the contented couples in this city. It was then I saw him. Him, my Master.

He was entering a shop in the center of town with a new young girl by his side. He gallantly held the door open for her, allowing her to enter first, then together they began to look at the evening dresses. It was then the young woman became angry. She raised her voice and stated that she wanted the leather miniskirt and the ankle boots, that she could no longer walk about in her present long skirt that made her look like a middle-aged woman. My Master tried to excuse her, tried to take hold of her hands, but she resisted him. The young girl was determined to cause a public scene. She turned and left my Master standing there in the middle of the store and walked out, muttering that she preferred to walk home on foot. It was only then that I began to understand what my eyes had just witnessed.

My Master was no longer my Master, in fact he was no longer the master of anything. He was only one of the many men who had chosen the wrong toy. A common mistake, particularly in a relationship of this kind, so different from ours. A relationship in which there were no similarities, only a gap, a distance that time would only make worse.

In fact, that young girl couldn't have been much more than twenty years old.

And my Master, on the other hand, would be forty next week.

WITHOUT MERCY

Erica Dumas

You promised to take me without mercy. I begged you for it, and now you're going to do it. And I'm scared. I'm so incredibly scared. I'm scared of giving in, I'm scared of resisting. I want it, and I've wanted it forever. But I'm scared.

You come up behind me and slip your arms around me, pressing the tip of the knife into my throat. I gasp and you say, "Don't scream." Then you growl into my ear, "Or I'll make you very sorry." Immediately my pussy floods with juice. You run the knife down my throat, the tip just barely touching me, and I moan softly in fear. You tease my lips open with the tip of it and I taste the sharp metal.

"Please," I whimper. "Please, no!"

You take the knife away from my mouth and close it. "I don't really need this, do I?" you whisper. "You know you can't stop me."

"Please," I moan. "Please don't rape me."

It sends a charge through my body, that word: *rape*. It makes my clit swell and throb hard against my panties. It makes my cunt clench even tighter. It makes me want you. But it makes me scared: the greatest terror a woman can know, and you're going to do it to me. Because I begged for it. Because I made you promise.

I say it again. "Please don't rape me," and my cunt aches, pain seizing my clit as it hardens so much my panties dig into it.

"That's exactly what I'm going to do," you whisper. "Rape you."

And I know it's true.

You force me hard into the bed and put your knee in the small of my back, holding me down as you tie my wrists behind me with rope.

"Please," I beg. "Please don't do this."

You ignore me and pull up my skirt. My panties are skimpy, small. I hear the knife again and in an instant you've slit them, pulling them out from between my legs so quickly that I feel the heat on my clit—panty burn. I gasp and push my ass into the air involuntarily. You hold me down.

"That's it," you growl as you stuff my shredded panties into my mouth. "Push your ass up for me. Beg for it."

I hear your zipper coming open. I feel the hard length of your cock slide against my ass, pressing between my cheeks. You mount me, forcing my legs open with your knees. I try to resist but you grab my hair, shove my face into the pillow and *force* them. So rough I'm afraid I'll pull a muscle, but I don't care. I struggle, but it's no use. Your hard, bunched thigh muscles push my legs wide open as I squirm.

Your hands go under my shirt and cup my breasts as you lower your body onto mine, the head of your cock pressing between my swollen lips. I gasp—now is the moment. Now is the moment I'd dreamed of. When my rape is inevitable, and when you realize I'm wet.

Not just wet: gushing.

You shove into me hard, so hard it would make me scream if I wasn't so desperately ready for it. I feel your cock going into me all the way, hitting my cervix with a rough push. But I don't scream. I don't scream at all: instead, I moan, the sound muffled by my wet, ruined panties.

I can't stop myself. I lift my ass to take you.

You pump into me, my pussy so tight around your cock, its blood vessels swollen with desire. I know I'm going to come and I fight it, more determined than I've ever been not to come—knowing that I don't have a choice. You fuck me hard, rough—without mercy. You slam into me, your hip bones striking my ass with each thrust. Your cock hitting the back of my pussy so hard that little shudders of pain go through my body with each surge of pleasure.

"No," I beg, what's left of my underwear hanging half out of my mouth. "No, no, no, no, no…" I say it over and over again, the word I've dreamed of, the litany I've fantasized about being able to say and know it will be absolutely ineffectual. And it is: it only makes you fuck me harder. But as I say it, over and over again: "No, no, no, no, no," it transforms—it no longer means "Don't rape me." It doesn't even mean "Don't fuck me." It means "Please, god, please, please, please, oh please don't make me come."

And that's when I do come, uncontrollably, my whole body shuddering, my pussy contracting around your pounding cock— the moment when I start to scream, loudest of all: "No! No! No! No! No!" I want to howl it: "Don't make me come, don't make me come," but I can't—I'm so far beyond words I can't say anything except, "No." So I scream it, over and over again, at the top of my lungs, not even caring if the neighbors call the cops. I scream it and thrash under you, struggling against the ropes that bind my wrists, fighting against the weight of your knees forcing my legs wide open. Resisting the pulse of your cock into me, making me come.

"Please," I whimper, as my orgasm trembles to a close. "Please, no, no, no, no..." It now means "Don't let me have just come. Please don't let me have just come." And that only makes me come harder, and whether it's a second orgasm or a resurgence of the first, I don't know. Sobs wrack my body as it explodes through me, and I hear you groaning, too, a bestial, violent sound, as you burst inside me and pump me full of your come. I struggle to stop pumping my ass with yours, fight to prevent my body from begging for it. But it's no use. I've been taken, subdued, overwhelmed. I've been forced by my own desire. I've been taken, without mercy.

But mercy is so overrated.

DIVORCE PROCEEDINGS

N. T. Morley

I'm three whiskeys into the evening, standing at the bar when she shows up looking immaculate in Bebe and Dolce & Gabbana. I know I look a little bit rumpled, but I barely even care. She's clutching the black leather valise that I bought her for graduation from law school.

I lean in and she kisses me on the cheek, coldly. I back off and gesture toward the nearby table.

"Can I get you something?" I ask, polishing off the remaining half of my whiskey.

"You're having another?"

"I know we're signing legal papers, but everything's settled, so I'd planned on it. That a problem?"

"Of course not. Vodka tonic," she says.

"Vodka tonic," I say with some amusement. Amanda rarely drinks, and when she does, she usually goes for wine.

She sits down, rummages through the valise, holds the papers facing her. I get a vodka tonic and another whiskey, sour this time, since drinking it straight's giving me a headache. I take the seat opposite her and smile.

"So, we're ready to finalize it," I say with a touch of sadness.

"Mike, I want to let you know, before you look at these papers, that I'm open to negotiation."

Her voice is shaking a little, which troubles me. Amanda is *never* nervous.

"I thought it was all settled," I tell her. "There's no real estate involved, I mean, you've got a car, I've got a car, community property is the Cole Porter boxed set and you already said I could have that." My voice gets an edge in it, and I can already feel myself losing control. "We talked about this, Mandy."

Her voice goes tight all of a sudden and even through my anger I can see she's never looked more beautiful. "Amanda," she says peevishly. "Please."

"Fine, then. A-man-da," I say, tightly, drawing her name out into a kind of snarky insult. "You make a hundred and twenty thousand freakin' dollars a year, Amanda, I work for the goddamned *Weekly* and play some jazz guitar on weekends for about a dollar seventy-five. What, do you think the *Times* is gonna secretly come through with that book deal they talked about in, oh, nineteen-ninety?"

Our eyes meet and her look freezes me to the core. "I know about Samara," she says.

"Oh, fuck," I say, groping for an explanation. "Listen, Amanda...I am so sorry about that."

I can't find the words.

"I was an asshole. There's...there's no excuse for cheating. It wasn't even—we didn't even have sex. I know that's no excuse, but I just want you to know that."

I'm trying to be cool, but inside, I'm freaking out—Amanda may not be a divorce lawyer, but she can bust balls with the best of them. If she wants to make my life unpleasant, I know, she'll have my underwear run up the flagpole by springtime. I want to ask her how she found out—but I know that'll just dig me a deeper grave.

She just looks at me, her expression cold.

"I'm sorry," I said. "I feel terrible."

"Actually," she says, "I'm not angry. That's why I want you to read these papers before you say any more. Because...well, just read the papers."

"Please," I beg her. "Please, Amanda, don't do this. If you ever loved me, don't make this any harder than it has to be."

"Read the papers, Mike."

"Please," I say. "I'm getting down on my knees."

"Mike, read the papers."

"I'm on my knees, Amanda. On my fucking knees. Begging you."

A little drunk, I'm actually dorky enough to push back my chair and get down on my knees, pressing my palms together in a gesture of pleading. Amanda glances around the bar with a disgusted look on her face. "I'm begging you. I'm down on my knees, Amanda."

"I noticed."

"Do you see me down on my knees? Begging you?"

She leans forward and hisses: "Mike, will you just read the fucking papers?"

I get up off my knees, brush off my rumpled suit and what little is left of my pride, and take my seat again while Amanda pushes the papers at me across the cocktail table.

I look at her pointedly before looking down.

"This is unethical," I say. I'm aware that my voice is slurring and it embarrasses me slightly, which makes it kind of stupid that I then repeat myself four, or maybe three and a half, times.

"Un-fucking-ethical, Amanda. Unethical, unethical, unethical."

Amanda rolls her eyes and then looks at me impatiently.

I take my reading glasses out of my coat pocket, put them on with a conscious flair.

AGREEMENT OF OWNERSHIP

Party of the first part, hereafter known as Mike, agrees with his signature below that henceforth he is owned entirely by party of the second part, hereafter known as Amanda. Mike relinquishes all rights of property and self-determination, including sexual self-determination, while Amanda accepts said rights over Mike.

Mike agrees that he will hereafter serve Amanda with the whole of his being, including both physical labor and sexual service of a type and frequency to be determined solely by Amanda. Physical and non-physical punishment will be meted out by Amanda at her sole discretion and for reasons she feels require it, or for no reasons at all.

I look at my wife, seeing her as nothing more than a blur through the narrow lenses of my reading glasses. Slowly I take the glasses off and open my mouth about six times before I manage to get a word out. Or, at least, a sound.

"Huh?"

"Sorry the language isn't quite legal," she says, her demeanor changing, suddenly familiar and even, maybe, flirtatious. "I was typing with one hand."

I'm on the verge of tears. Fucking bitch, for ridiculing me like this, after all we put each other through.

"This is a really fucking cruel joke," I say to her.

I know Amanda's expressions, and this one is dead serious, even with that twisted smile on one half of her face.

"If it was a joke," she told me, "I'd have had it sent over by courier."

"You're serious?"

"Read the rest of it," she says.

I put my reading glasses back on and slowly make my way through the rest of the agreement. Details are spotty, and there are quite a few typos when she gets into the heart of things.

I glance around the table, then clear my throat.

"This paragraph about butt plugs," I say.

Her eyes are smoky as she looks at me, leans across the table, puts one hand on mine.

"Mmmmm-hmmmm?" she asks, her face flushing slightly.

"It doesn't specify a size," I say. "And just for the record, butt—"

"Yes, I know *butt* has two *T*s in it," says Amanda, her voice low. "And I'll decide what size you can take."

That makes me shift uncomfortably in my seat, and I read the rest of the agreement with Amanda's long fingernail tracing designs on the back of my hand.

I take a deep breath, which is much more challenging than it sounds, under the circumstances. With the hand my wife isn't stroking, I loosen my tie, polish off my drink, and gesture at the cocktail waitress. She makes an eye gesture at Amanda, and I glance at my wife, who eyeballs her vodka tonic, still half-full.

I shake my head and the cocktail waitress gestures *okay* at me with thumb and forefinger. I turn back to Amanda, finding myself unable to speak for a few minutes.

She just lets me flounder, never taking her eyes off of me,

doubtless making note of the reddening of my face under her pressuring gaze.

"Well," I say, "I guess this means you're keeping Cole Porter."

"Don't be cute," she says. "It doesn't become you."

I shrug. "I don't know what to say, Amanda."

"Are you hard right now?" she asks softly.

I look left, look right, glance behind me.

I nod.

"Then say, 'Yes.' "

"This is a big step. We separated six months ago."

"So you've moved on with your life."

"No, but I was looking forward to being able to."

"I don't believe that any more than you do."

"Amanda...this is weird. Why are you doing this?"

Amanda sighs, removes her hand from mine, sits back in her seat.

"Six months is a long time, Mike," she says. "I've learned things about myself. And I think I've realized some things about you."

My heart pounds. "Oh? What did you learn about me?"

"I think you already know."

My words are measured, my voice quavering. "You say you've learned things about yourself," I say. "I think I can guess what that means."

"And you'd probably make a pretty good guess."

I look at the agreement.

"I need to think about this."

Amanda purses her lips.

"Can I?" I ask her. "Can I think about this? I mean, this is a lot to take in."

"I certainly can't tell you what to do. Yet."

"That's comforting," I say.

"But I'm going to give you three good reasons why I don't think you should think about this at all."

"First...I've already forgiven you for Mistress Samara."

"You know, I'm so sorry about that, I really just want to say—"

She talks over me, raising her voice just enough to shut me up. "And there's a very good chance that I'll forget that I've forgiven you—if you make me wait."

"Sure you will, little Miss 'I've learned things about myself.'"

With a roll of her eyes, she goes on, louder than before, and I lapse into silence. "Second, you're slightly drunk right now, and I think this safe, sane, and consensual stuff may apply to whips and chains, but I'll be fucking well damned if it applies to divorce. I'd like you a little drunk, because I think you're too proud and too stupid to admit what you want without a few whiskeys inside you."

As if on cue, the cocktail waitress shows up, a punked-out college student looking awfully funky in a white blouse and black skirt.

"Can I get you anything else?" she asks, nervously, picking up on the tension in the air.

Amanda never looks up; she just stares at me, our eyes locked. I glance at the cocktail waitress and say softly, "No, thanks, this'll do it."

"Should I bring the check?" Amanda's eyebrows go up. Meekly, I nod.

"Yes, please," says Amanda, evenly, without looking up. The cocktail waitress disappears.

"That wasn't a 'yes,' " I say. "I still want to know the third reason."

Her voice was low and husky: "The third reason you're going to say yes is that I'm so fucking horny right now I'm going to chew the veneer off this fucking table. If you aren't going to sign the goddamn thing, for god's sake at least take me home and fuck me for old time's sake."

I think about it for a moment.

"My place is closer," I say.

"I know that."

"I don't have a bed."

"Do you have a floor?"

"I've heard rumors."

"Then call a cab."

"I thought you were sober."

"But not in any condition to drive," she says, and picks up her valise.

Our first kiss happens in the back of the cab, in a spiraling, swerving traffic war up Market Street. I would say it's our first kiss in six months, but for real kisses it's been much longer—nine, ten, eleven months; a year, two years, five. Her tongue hasn't tasted this sweet since the first time we made love.

"What does 'Sexual service of a type and frequency to be determined solely by Amanda' mean?" I murmur between kisses.

She thrusts her body against mine, seizing my balls deftly through wool blend and cotton.

"It means I own these," she whispers, and her finger comes sliding up to pop in my mouth, caressing my tongue. "And I own this. Probably more importantly," she whispers as she begins to nuzzle my ear, two fingers deep in my mouth, and by the time she slides them out, my cock, having for a moment gone into make-out session demi-tumescence, is rock hard again. "But then, I own all of you," she sighs, her lips caressing my earlobe. She deftly unbuttons one button of the dress shirt and her hand goes into it, tweaking a nipple through the wife-beater. "I own these," she says. "And this," and as I squirm she removes her hand from my shirt and drops it between my legs, caressing my cock. "And," she whispers, with some difficulty wedging her hand under my crotch so she can grab my ass, right in the middle, the pressure coaxing a gasp out of me. "You already know I own your ass." She laughs softly into my ear. "Remember that night in Carmel?"

She's referring, we both know, to probably the last really mind-blowing sex Amanda and I enjoyed together. It was a weekend away in Carmel, two years ago...maybe three. Before I started seeing Mistress Samara. Before things went bad between us.

Amanda was giving me a blow job on the clean, starched hotel sheets, and right in the middle of it, when I was moaning and ready to come, she licked her finger and slid it into my ass. I came so hard I took the lord's name in vain, and several other deities, as well. Neither Amanda nor I ever mentioned it again.

"What 'things' did you realize about me?" I ask her, my voice suddenly serious.

"Crap, Michael, stop being such a process queen," she growls, still groping my ass. "We're almost there. There'll be plenty of time for twenty questions after you fuck me bowlegged."

Upstairs, she drops the valise and slams me against the wall before the door's even closed—or maybe I slam her, it's all very confused. With a kick to the door and an audible thunk, we're finally inside my tiny studio, discarded Styrofoam takeout containers and already-ruined CD cases crunching under my loafers and Amanda's pumps. The smell is musty, ripe.

"Let me light some incense," I tell her.

"No," she says, and trips me onto the mattress.

"You do so have a bed," she says, coming down on top of me and straddling me, her businesslike navy-blue skirt riding up onto her thighs and showing me the lace tops of her stockings, hitched to black satin garters.

She rips open my shirt, not even bothering with the tie. A single button skids across the floor as Amanda seizes my hand.

"It's not a bed," I plead. "It's a mattress."

She wedges my hand between her thighs, under her skirt, and presses my fingers into her. She leans back on me, legs spread, back arching, a long, low moan coming out of her as my fingers go deep inside. She's smooth, and wet enough that after a few thrusts a little stream of moisture dribbles down onto my wrist. She loses the jacket while she rides my hand, and her blouse loses two buttons, maybe three, as she rips it open.

Then she comes forward onto me, hard, slamming my hand between us and shoving her own into the remains of my shirt. Her sharp fingernails rake my skin, and this time it's my turn to moan. She leaves deep red furrows, I know without looking— have to, because my eyes are shut tight and my head thrown back so far my face is buried in the stinking pillow. She rakes me again and I thrash, no longer able to keep my fingers inside her. Violently, I claw at the rumpled mattress, and the corner of the contour sheet hits me on the side of my face.

I look up at her just in time to feel her fingernails rake me again, and this time I don't throw my head back, don't bury my face in the pillow—in fact, I don't look away at all. Her eyes, fiery, hold mine and she looks deep as she shreds my chest, making me bleat in pain.

As her fingernails dig in, I grab her wrists, gasping up at her. "Please," I beg.

"Oh," she says, as if coming out of a daze. "We didn't de-cide on a safeword, did we?" I shake my head emphatically, and when she opens her mouth to speak again, I shake my head again. "You're sure?" I nod.

She really has changed—she understands, in the same way

we understood each other over most of eight years—but on a complicated topic we've never discussed. *I don't need a fucking safeword*, I might have told her if I had been able. *Because you fucking own me, so fuck it.* But I can't say that, something in the saying of it would carry the weight of shame and secrecy, and that stops me every time—stopped me for two years, three, maybe four before it finally broke us apart. But Amanda, alone among the creatures on earth, can read my eyes and know what I'm thinking. And what I'm thinking is, *Please.*

But I can't keep my mouth shut; the question bubbles out of me as I struggle against her.

"Take your hands away," she growls. I grip her wrists, still preventing her from raking my chest again.

"I need to know," I tell her. "I need to know that you're not just doing this for me."

She wrenches her hands free, pushes herself off of me. She rises from the bed and looks at me, her gaze cold. She pulls down her navy blue skirt, smoothes it over her thighs. She pulls her blouse closed.

Amanda walks toward the door.

Fuck, I think. *You spoiled it. One last hot fuck with your ex-wife, it turns out she's gone all kinky, and you have to blow it by getting all processy.*

I open my mouth to say something, but there's nothing to say. I blew it. I should have taken what was offered, and not questioned her motives. A free fuck from a horny ex-wife is hardly an offer from a loan shark.

I close my eyes. I can't bear to see her walk out the door.

But the door doesn't open, and her pumps make click-click-crunch sounds across hardwood and shattered plastic and back again, and when I open my eyes she's standing over me with the valise in her hand.

She sets it down, upright, and shrugs off her blouse. Her breasts are as lovely as ever, spilling out of a white push-up bra, and I remember in a rush every taste I've had of them—every touch, every caress, every bead of sweat I've lipped off those perfect nipples. The skirt goes down with a zip and a wriggle, pooling around her ankles. It's only when she steps out of it that I realize what should have been obvious before: she wasn't wearing anything underneath.

She goes down on one knee, reaches into the valise. Her hand comes out with a flogger. She rises, slowly, and reaches back to unfasten her hair.

She shakes it out with one hand, swirling the flogger with the other so that a breeze wafts my way. It's a heavy weapon—bull hide, probably, or maybe buckskin. She snaps the flogger in the air, lets it hang at her side, succulent and menacing. The scent of the leather reaches my nostrils, and my cock, gone once again demi-tumescent, this time with process anxiety, is hard before the second whiff.

"When I'm doing something for you," she says, rising slowly, "you'll know." Another snap of the flogger. "Because Hell will have just frozen over," she tells me.

I tear the rest of my clothes off in about five seconds flat, and she's on me, then, with flogger and fingernails, her open palm striking my reddening ass, her fingers circling around my balls and squeezing till I wail.

It's familiar, the pain—and that hurts me to know; in the midst of it, I want to cry out apologies, blurt out explanations, find the words for why I know the pain, administered by another's hand, more intimately than I know the taste of my wife's sex.

But every time I go to speak, she reacquaints me with the former, with flogger and bare palm—and by the time she's done with that, she's reacquainting me with the latter, her weight upon me, her thighs spread around my face and her hand tangled in my hair, holding me in place while she fucks my mouth, savagely, until she comes. Then, relinquishing her grip on me for a few minutes, she rolls sweaty and panting into a sheet-tangled semi-slumber as the angle of the autumn sunlight changes outside my apartment's single window and fades finally, ominously, to black.

When I hear the whisper of a snore coming from her, I get out of bed and put on my clothes in the darkness.

She awakens as I start putting the last shelf of books into a file box. She peers into what's left of the moonlight, the only illumination.

"I didn't want to wake you," I tell her.

"What the hell are you doing?"

"I'm packing my books," I said. "It's on the nightstand."

"What is?"

I don't answer her. Putting another handful of paperbacks in the box, I refrain from looking over as she discovers that by "nightstand," I mean "overturned milk crate," and by "it" I mean our contract, signed, which she probably can't see in the darkness, anyway. I don't look over because I can't bear to see her face, can't take the chance that I'll see an expression of regret on it, an "Oh, brother" that means, now that she's not quite so horny and remembers what a bore I am in bed, this all turned out to be a shitty idea.

But I can't stand the silence. I finally do look over at her, and while her eyes aren't yet fully adjusted to the darkness, mine are. I can see her clutching the wrinkled contract to her naked chest.

"You're not angry at Samara, I hope?"

I know, then, for sure, why it is that Amanda knows my every kink; why she understands what I've wanted all these years, without being able to admit I want it, even, or especially, to my-self. I knew it before, or maybe more than suspected it, from the instant Amanda first grabbed my balls and squeezed, or maybe the moment I realized that the flogger was bull's hide, all thud and little sting, or perhaps the instant I heard her whisper "I own these," into my ear, all of which seemed too conveniently tailored for a world in which I am utterly happy.

The business with the fingernails threw me, though—that was pure Amanda, as much her trademark as that black leather valise. I could still feel the sting every time I moved my arms.

The rest of it was pure Samara, pure Mike, my personal kinks mingled with her admirable skills; I had been in the hands of what could be nothing other—it seemed obvious now—than a gifted apprentice.

It's the most egregious violation of pro-dom protocol, of professional ethics in a world where ethics are the only thing between most of us and madness. This was apostasy, pure and simple, the most extreme blasphemy in the land of perversion.

It's a small community, though, and shit happens. How-ever Samara encountered the newly-coming-out divorcée—Play party? Munch? Session?—and heard her side of the story, her normally impeccable ethics must have seemed of secondary importance to the very real possibility that Amanda and I had been about to costar in a very real and very perverted back-alley production of "Gift of the Magi." *His name's Mike Southern,* Amanda might have said, *he writes for the* Weekly. *Jesus fuck-ing Christ,* Samara told her, maybe. *Just beat the shit out of him, will you? You'll both be glad you did.*

"I want to buy her a Lexus," I sigh.

"Too bad you lost everything in the divorce."

"Fuck it," I tell her. "I only had one thing that mattered, anyway. I just didn't know it."

I hear her vague sigh of contentment, oddly rapturous, strangely romantic from one who had so recently finished making me bleed.

"Then come to bed," says the Mistress.

So I do.

Amanda, as it turns out, is *not* finished making me bleed.

WELL TRAINED

Alison Tyler

My men have always been vice afflicted. Sleek to the bone with insomniacs' purple smudges under their eyes. You know the type. Pool hall junkies. Bartending actors. Razor sharp, they've owed their delectably hard bodies to the debauchery of espresso and cigarette breakfasts at noon, not an unnatural devotion to treadmills before dawn.

Until Granger.

When I caught sight of him at a birthday party for a friend, I noted his shaved head and his lean, foxy face and thought, *Just my type.* I didn't know that the drink in his hand was imported water, not imported vodka. Didn't know that his chiseled good looks came from hours of training sloths with no willpower rather than from forgoing three square meals in favor of a double shot of Johnny Walker and a Marlboro Red. I didn't need someone to critique my lifestyle, to throw out my beloved Froot Loops in favor of bland rabbit food, to try and pinch an inch on my waist, or anywhere else. My years of bad habits have made me who I am—and I will change for no man. Marlena claims this is why I'm single. In general, unless I'm feeling particularly lonely, I ignore her.

"Handsome, isn't he?" Marlena asked. She'd caught me flirting.

"And then some," I agreed.

"So sign up."

"There's a waiting list to fuck him?" I could feel the smile meet my eyes.

"No, to train with him," she explained to my horror. "His name is Granger and he owns Rush, the gym on Fourth Street." I'd been hoodwinked. He didn't look like a trainer—not my idea of one, anyway. Sure, he had a tight body in his simple black cashmere sweater and well-cut gray slacks, but he didn't appear overly muscle-bound. There were no rippling biceps, no Mr. America inverted-triangle-shaped physique, top-heavy upper body tapering to a tiny, girlish waist. I couldn't imagine him gleaming bronze beneath bright white lights, striking pose after pose for an audience of hooting female fans.

As I watched, he casually stroked the lower back of the red-haired woman at his side. She was wearing a formfitting emerald dress with an oval cutout that dipped dangerously low in the rear. I could see her structured arms, her superior posture, the way she seemed to radiate an inner strength.

Was this luminous woman a girlfriend, a client, or both?

I stared, transfixed, as his fingers lingered again at the lowest point of the dress, more forcefully this time. At his touch, she turned automatically to face him, as if well trained. An image flickered in my mind—an image of him in worn black leather and me at his side, not in a dress, but stripped totally bare, not standing as his equal, but on my knees on the floor at his feet—then immediately that vision was gone.

"I'm no gym rat," I reminded Marlena, losing interest. "I don't do trainers." The thought of discussing whey-shakes and tight glutes made me nauseous.

"Break your rules," she advised. "And try this one."

I shook my head, my shiny black bob swinging gently over my cheeks. Sure I live in California, but I'm not nutty *or* crunchy. And although I am acquainted with people who jog, I've never been a fan of the pink-cheeked glow of health that comes from excessive physical activity. When I see studs pumping iron out at Muscle Beach, I turn my head away from their glistening, sweat-drenched figures—not in heart-pounding lust, but in embarrassment. They look like nothing more than caged animals behind the cool silver wrought-iron fence, steroid-enhanced freaks putting on a show for the masses.

"He's a total sadist, you know," she added gleefully, her eyes still focused on Granger's handsome visage. I stared at her, incredulous. She'd said my buzzword.

"What do you mean?" I tried to hide the excitement in my voice.

"There's no other possible excuse," she continued, now turning to face me. "He loves punishing women. Pushing them to their very limits, demolishing every last bit of their sense of self before building them up from scratch again." And now she laughed, drunkenly, and tossed her blonde shoulder-length curls in her look-at-me way that tends to get her what—and *who*—she wants.

Did she know? Could she guess?

When I stared harder at her, I realized that she had no idea what her whispered giggly confession had done to me. I looked back at Granger, deeply curious.

I go for hoodlums and dark horses, men who have the strength to take me beyond my boundaries. I like after-hours clubs, black velvet, dark smoky places. After being in charge all day long, I like to give myself over to someone else. To someone who knows, who understands the urges that live within me. Brightly lit rooms equipped with shiny gym equipment and floor-to-ceiling mirrored walls do nothing for my libido.

But *sadist*—she'd called him that. And as I looked over at him again, I felt his cold blue eyes returning the appraisal. I considered what he was seeing. My body is slender and toned, but not from hours climbing walls or walking moveable, gray, rubberized tracks to nowhere. I simply can't be bothered with the guilt that always accompanies a gym membership, and the inevitable failure to use it. My lifestyle is workout enough, slamming myself up against deadline after deadline. When the health freaks all did Tae Bo, I had Thai food. When the new rage was yoga performed in a hellishly hot room, I took a relaxing sauna. I'll admit to a single run-in with a gym rat, way back in high school, a man who could bench-press three of me if he'd wanted to. A man who couldn't comfortably bend his arms all the way because the bulges of muscles interfered. It was amusing to watch him try to eat soup, the bicep rippling as he attempted to bring spoon to mouth. It was amusing being bench-pressed, quite honestly, but when that turned out to be his one and only party trick, I lost interest...and found interest in the guys who hung out *behind* the gym—the stoners and slackers and goth writers who wore all black. The motorcycle mavericks who favored faded denim and beaten-in leather. I developed a taste for beer and smoke on the lips of my lovers. What would I possibly do with someone who liked neon-green wheatgrass juice and freshly blanched almond paste?

Or rather, what would *he* do with someone like me?

Yet I found myself staring, calculating, considering. It had been a good long while since my last relationship. And who was saying anything here about a relationship at all? Fucking a trainer was different from dating one, right? I'm strong willed. I could keep my sense of self intact. I wouldn't be like the girl at his side, the one who moved her body at the silent instruction of his fingertips. The one who seemed invisibly connected to him, so that when he maneuvered her attention, she followed like a lapdog, pivoting at his every unspoken command.

Well trained, I thought again, accidentally meeting his eyes a second time.

Could he tell what I was thinking? Did he look at me as a challenge—me with my Ketel One martini in hand and plate of rich appetizers at my side? When he nodded in my direction, giving me a sharp smile behind his date's back, was he seeing something to be tamed, something to be broken? I couldn't tell. I could only hope.

Near the end of the party, he made his way to my side and offered a hand in greeting. I took it, and we stood there, sizing each other up like athletes before a competition. There was a heat between us, palpable and real, and although I doubted even the possibility of a successful one-night love connection, I found myself dialing up the number for Rush the next week.

Just on a lark, I assured myself. Just to see.

Marlena was right. He liked pushing women. From the start, he had me out of bed three hours earlier than my usual de-molishing of the alarm clock against the wall. Three fucking hours, I might say. I balked at the five a.m. appointment, ex-plaining that I'm often up until dawn working, but he assured me that I'd have far more energy after training with him than I'd ever had before. When I showed up bleary eyed with a to-go cup of rich, dark coffee in hand, he tossed my half-finished cup in the trash and shook his shaved head, disappointed.

Rather than arguing with him, I found myself wanting to show him that I could do it, that I had it in me. I took his gaze as a challenge.

At least, I did until he started the workout.

Nothing could have prepared me for the pain. Nor for the way he dismissed the pain with a little half-smile, as if he were immune. As if the screaming agony of my poor muscles was nothing more than a little twinge of discomfort. I would have quit after one set of crunches, but I kept hearing Marlena's voice in my head: *Sadist. He's a total sadist.*

Was he one outside of the gym? That's what I desperately wanted to know.

So I played along, and I found myself striving harder to win his approval. When he shot a disparaging look at my battered gray pants, I traded those beloved college sweats for a pair of fitted black Lycra leggings. When he sarcastically queried how I could still be alive based on my irredeemable choices of food, I followed his carefully prepared diet, forgoing my favorite comfort meals for stone-cut oatmeal, freshly grilled wild salmon, egg-white omelets with baby spinach. I started to feel the burn, started to actually understand the concept of a runner's high. And I thought I felt something else, as well. When he trained me, his hand would linger on the small of my back, on the inside of my thigh, or on the curve of my waist. He'd position me just so, and then the professionalism would fade, and I'd feel a squeeze, or a touch or the softest pat.

Was it encouragement only, or was he interested?

Something in me started to change. Yes, I was crushing on this man, but I also became enamored of the sensations ricocheting through me. I did have more energy. He was right about that. Dark, smoky clubs started to feel just like they looked: dark and smoky. Why would anyone want to be trapped in one of those places rather than spend hours in a clean, well-lit, healthy environment in the company of other clean, well-lit, healthy people? My skin glowed. My brown eyes were brighter than they had been in years. Friends noticed a change in my appearance, and I noticed that my clothes started to fit me differently. I've always been slim. Now, I was hard. Addiction set in before I was truly aware of what had happened.

I began going to the gym on days Granger wasn't training me, just to work out on my own—amazingly finding that I truly missed it if I skipped a day. And when I watched him from the elliptical machine, surreptitiously viewing the way he behaved with other clients, I realized that he didn't seem to touch the other women the way he touched me—his fingertips light, the tingle of sweat and lust keeping me ever off balance. He maintained a distance with the others that I reveled in. It was me he was interested in. *Me* he wanted.

Finally, at the end of one session, he bent to whisper in my ear, "We'll have a night lesson next."

"Night lesson?"

"Meet me here at eleven."

The gym closed at ten. This was going to be different. This was what I'd been waiting for. I knew it. And I was right.

He didn't do anything out of the ordinary at first. Nothing noticeable, anyway. He didn't tell me to strip out of my clothes so that he could work me out naked, or whisper that he wanted to fuck me up against the red vinyl slanted board, the site of my countless nightmarish sit-ups. Instead, he moved me through my regular routine, perhaps being slightly stricter than usual, forcing me to hold the weights longer, to breathe slower.

But then, as we neared the end, as my heart raced and my blood pumped at a rapid pace, he put one strong hand on my thigh. My whole body quivered at his touch. His fingers slid between my legs, pressing against my Lycra-clad pussy as I lowered the gleaming silver barbell.

"Don't stop," Granger hissed, and I took a breath and forced myself to do yet another rep. And another. This time, his fingertips slid in a smooth circle, touching my clit as I trembled all over. I watched his eyes in the mirror, rather than my own. Their blue was arctic, icy, and they froze me to my place.

"Concentrate," he insisted. "Come on, girl. Don't slack off now."

A hiss of air escaped from between my clenched teeth.

"Don't look at me, baby—" *Baby. He called me baby. Like all my other hard-core lovers. Like the men in black leather, not black Lycra.* "—watch yourself."

With effort, I met my own gaze in the mirror and I did my best. One, two, three, four, five, up. Then four beats down, a little faster.

"Do it again, darling. Do it again."

Darling now, was it? *Darling* and *baby* and my muscles were shaking uncontrollably. This was like being tied down. This was like fucking on the floor of my tiny apartment. This was like a belt in the air—

"Don't let me down."

No, I didn't want to let him down. Not now. Not ever.

One, two, three, four—oh, god, he was touching my clit just right. So nice. My arms were trembling. His eyes were like ice in the mirror, frozen blue. Colder than cold. *Don't stop. Don't stop concentrating.*

He was training me. Training me in a whole new way. And this was something I could understand. *These* were the lessons I'd longed for.

We continued back at his apartment. He didn't change the method of his training. He only changed the genre. His voice was that same, fierce bark. His eyes held that same disapproving look when I failed to properly complete a task. Only now, we were alone. There were no others to see my downfall. No mirrors to reflect my transgressions into dizzying infinity. Now, he punished me in different ways. Not by forcing me to do an extra rep when my muscles were already screaming in agony—but by forcing me to bend over the sleek desk in his home office, to grit my teeth and wait for the sting of his leather belt on my naked skin.

He was a sadist. That was the truth. But I'd never known a sadist could live outside of the world that I inhabited. I hadn't known there were healthy vegan sadists; that there were men who knew how to take charge who didn't ride Harleys or hot rods, who didn't sport tattoos or scars from long-ago wipeouts.

Granger was one. He proved all my stereotypes wrong. And in a month, he had me well trained.

Trained to come when he called.

Trained to crawl across his apartment on my hands and knees. Trained to lower my eyes when he spoke my name in a certain tone. Trained to climax when astride his lap, facing my own reflection as he thrust his greased-up cock into my asshole, his fingers strumming my tender clit so that we reached our limits together.

His body was unbelievable. He could pick me up, position me, hold me exactly how he wanted to—just like that other gym rat so long ago. But this was different. I wasn't a weight to be pressed. I was a force to be possessed, a tangible energy to be bent and molded.

When we worked out together in the gym, I thought about how it felt when he fucked me. When he fucked me, I thought about him forcing me to do another crunch at the gym. "One more, baby. Come on, just one more." The two actions became synonymous in my head: working out and fucking. Being worked out and being fucked. On a solo run through the Hollywood Hills, I imagined him at my side, hissing orders, forcing me on past my limits, a leather belt doubled in his hand. In his bed, with my wrists cuffed tightly to the metal railing, I pictured myself doing another rep, always just one more rep, feeling my muscles shriek in protest, forcing myself to hit one more mark.

Both situations made me equally wet.

Granger had twisted everything up inside of me. Looking at my gym bag was foreplay. Staring at the weights he kept at home made me twist in my seat. I was ready for him all the time, but he liked waiting for it, forcing me through excruciating lessons before allowing himself to fuck me. He never seemed to lose his cool, even at our most heated moments. It was as if he had an icy core, one that showed only in his eyes and in his voice. He was never out of breath. Never mussed. Never shaken. I had faith in this quality of his. I bowed down before it.

"You're not trying," he said sometimes, and those were the words that made me feel the worst. All he asked from me was everything. I would have sweated blood to give to him. Whenever I questioned my abilities, I'd look into his eyes and find the strength to go forward. To prove myself to him. To win his praise.

I lost myself in the endorphin rush. I felt sleek and pure, given over both to the healthy attitude of being a gym rat, and the runner's high of being well trained.

And then, as athletics junkies occasionally do, I allowed myself to start to relax—both about my workouts and about my man. Granger was mine. I could tell. He was different with me. He was tender with me, even through the pain, or maybe *because* of the pain. Oh, was he tender.

I started to let down my guard, even to cheat every once in

a while. Cheat on the prescribed diet he'd written out for me, choosing an espresso over a white tea, a Reese's Peanut Butter Cup over a handful of hateful trail mix. I cheated on the intensity of my workouts, as well, stopping after two sets of ten reps rather than three, knocking off five minutes early when I was working out on my own. As if sensing this shift within me, Granger suddenly called to beg off my morning appointments. "This week's a bitch," he explained in his clipped tone. "I have to shuffle everything around to fit in a new client. Take a few days off. Give yourself a reward. Sleep in."

I did so for nearly a week, reveling in bad old habits. Letting sunshine wake me rather than the scream of an alarm. I expected my body to respond with glee—but it didn't. Instead, I looked at my forlorn gym bag with distress. Granger had trained me, and I had trained myself, to want to see sunrise when I left the gym, sweaty and happy, vibrating with the swirl of endorphins. So after five days off, I decided to show up predawn, as I had for so many weeks previously. I missed the way my body had ached all day. I missed the blinding pain that came right before the pleasure.

When I walked in the gym it was like walking in on two lovers. Surrounded by that healthy, brightly lit glow, the mirrored walls, the highly polished equipment, I felt my heart throb in my chest, as if I had just completed a ten-mile run when all I'd done was catch his eye in the mirror.

Sadist.

Marlena had said it. But she hadn't known. Hadn't comprehended.

Sadist.

I saw it. His blue eyes gleaming. His muscles pumped.

His hand on someone else's thigh.

RECUERDOS AGRIDULCES

Sophia Valenti

I'll never forget the first time I made Antonio cry.

The night we met, he strode into the room acting as if he owned the place. In truth, if he didn't he could have easily snatched it up. He was as wealthy as he was arrogant. He always got what he wanted and never heard no—until he met me.

He was a colleague of a friend of mine, and while he didn't live in my city, he was a frequent visitor because of his business responsibilities. Lily thought we'd be a perfect match and insisted we meet. Quite honestly, she knew nothing about me, but she was a nice girl, so I thought I'd humor her. But she was right. Antonio and I *were* quite a match—but not in the way she'd anticipated. I'm sure she was expecting hearts and flowers, but when he and I got together, it was more like throwing kerosene on a fire.

After Lily made her introductions, she conveniently disappeared, her smug smile assuring me that she was certain she'd orchestrated a love connection. There was a connection all right—fifteen minutes later we were rolling around on his hotel room bed.

As soon as we'd stumbled through the threshold, he was on me. His kisses were aggressive, and his hands went straight for my panties, smoothly slipping them down my hips and off my high-heeled feet. I fought back, tearing at his clothes with the same feral impatience. While my dress remained on, he was soon completely naked on the bed. His caramel-colored skin was cool, his body nearly hairless. As I straddled him, I stroked my nails down his chest, leaving red streaks behind as I raked his flesh. A hiss escaped his lips, and I saw a glimmer of hesitation in his dark eyes. Moments ago, those eyes had smoldered with the lustful heat of a man intent on his next conquest, but now they revealed a hint of obsequiousness—along with a bit of hope. That look stoked my libido more than the sight of his stiff cock ever could.

We tumbled around on the bed, but I made sure I wound up on top. I took hold of his hands and raised them. "The headboard—grab it. And don't you dare let go," I told him, releasing him and watching him obediently thread his fingers through the brass curlicues. He flexed his fingers a few times and licked his lips, looking unsure, but his unflagging erection told me that I was on the right track.

"Why?" he finally asked, his voice raspy.

I slapped him across the face—not harshly, but hard enough to get his attention. His eyes grew wide, yet I felt his cock pulse beneath me.

"Never question me. Do you understand?"

"Y-yes."

The bold businessman who'd bossed around the cocktail waitress was gone. I bit my lip to hide the smile that was threatening to spread across my face; he was already mine.

"Yes, *what?*" I toyed with him, wondering if he'd take the bait—wondering if my suspicions were correct.

"Yes, Mistress," he whispered. He averted his gaze, and I felt my desire for him increase tenfold.

I raised my hips slightly, grabbing his dick at the base, and then sinking myself down onto him. I was so hot and wet that his cock slid into me with ease, despite his substantial heft. When I hit bottom, I ground my body against his, enjoying the exquisite friction against my clit. Each snap of my hips swiped it in just the right way, and I continued writhing like that until I sparked my climax. I gasped, and my cunt spasmed around his thick shaft as he moaned. After I rode out the final wave of my pleasure, I climbed off him, leaving his shiny erection bobbing in the air, and then straightened my dress and grabbed my purse.

"I'll see you here tomorrow night. Seven o'clock."

"For what?" he asked, incredulously.

My mouth curled upward in an irrepressible smirk. "To punish you, for one thing. You were told not to question me."

"I'm sorry, ma'am," he whispered.

"You will be." I turned and left.

The next night he was waiting for me in his room, looking humble and contrite. It made me want him even more than I already did.

I came prepared for our second date, bringing along some toys, including my favorite leather slapper—its bark was as bad as its bite. I spread him across my lap, slotting his cock between my bare thighs. He jumped at the first strike, moaning as I simultaneously squeezed his shaft—a touch of sweetness to temper the sting. I used the stiff leather to stripe his cheeks, enjoying the sound of his gasps each time I laid down another layer of heat. At one point his hips began to rise and fall rhyth-mically, but I grabbed his hair and tugged his face toward me, so I could look into his eyes.

"Don't forget your place, Antonio. I control your cock—not you."

"I-I'm sorry, ma'am. It's just—"

"I know, honey, but I'm not done with you yet."

I nudged him off my knees and told him to stand before me. He did so immediately, and I walked around him, noting the goose bumps that had risen on his flesh and admiring the becoming blush that covered his lower cheeks.

Leaning forward, I tongued his nipples until they were stiff enough for me to clamp. I applied alligator clips to each nub, tightening the clamps until he gasped, and then I yanked on the chain that attached them to bring him to his knees. I sat on the edge of the bed and spread my legs; he didn't wait for an order to dive between my thighs. His tongue expertly swirled around my clit and plunged inside my hole. I tugged harshly on the chain as the vibrations from his groans took me to the brink. I looked down at him, his tongue not stopping the slip-sliding motions that were filling me with bliss, even though his eyes were glistening and a tear was running down his cheek. The sight melted my heart.

I think that's the moment I fell in love.

We carried on like that for months, with me pushing him to take more and more, and him doing just that, every single time. His willingness to please and his hunger for punishment were like nothing I'd ever seen. I found that I could easily satisfy his lust, his desire to submit, but that was all I had to give.

Eventually, the demands of his business kept him overseas more and more, and his visits decreased in frequency. He demanded that I go home to Europe with him, but I told him no.

I cared for him—I really did—but not in that way.

During his last visit, he begged me one final time to go with him. I refused, and his eyes overflowed with tears as he said good-bye.

I'll never forget the last time I made Antonio cry. Because I cried, too.

A SECRET KING

Sommer Marsden

'll admit that it took me a good week to get used to hearing Jared say Daddy. The first time he said it I swore he meant daddy as in sugar. I figured what I had before me in the flashing, booming bar was a man-whore. A pretty, charming man-whore.

Wrong. Looks can be deceiving and so can first impressions. What I had was a good old boy who called his father one of two things. Daddy or sir. A man schooled in the ways of quiet self assurance and respect.

When I got him home that night, again I figured that I had one of two things…a man who didn't know a clit from a cocktail straw or a guy who'd just bang one out and ask if I had a beer. Wrong again.

What I had was a bit of a dominant who trussed me to the bed with his big leather belt and fucked me blue. He made me beg him for things I didn't know I wanted, until I considered calling *him* Daddy. *Then* he asked me if I had any beer.

Two months had passed and Jared and I had been insepa-rable. He announced to me that he had to talk to Daddy about something and I was coming with him.

"What if I don't want to go?" I asked.

He backed me to the bed post and had my good silk stocking wrapped around my wrists before I could even blink. "What if you don't?" he asked, almost conversationally. That always pushed me into rose-red lust. The nonchalant way he had of telling me what I would do.

"What if I don't?" I said again because I couldn't think of what else to say. All I could really focus on was the sensual bite of silk stockings pressing into my skin and the way he kneed my legs open so he could run his finger along the split of my sex. I was still in jeans, but I bet he knew I was wet. His smile said he knew.

"Then I guess you don't have to *come*." He almost kissed me then, my ears picking up his deliberate accent on the final word of his sentence. His breath feathered across my bottom lip. I felt that hitch in my chest, that excitement that uncoiled low in my gut like a curl of smoke. But at the very last second he pulled back and left me very much unkissed.

"Jared." I begged with just that one word.

"Maybe I can convince you that you want to come," he chuckled.

His big fingers didn't look like they would work on such a tiny brass button, but he had me out of my jeans pretty fast. His fingers, warm and blunt and used to hard work—on a farm of all places—slipped into my pussy. He flexed the fingertips roughly and his touch shot straight to that moist, secret place in me that craved him the most. He played my G-spot like a man playing a piano he'd played for years.

The orgasm that I wanted desperately rubbed up against me,

and I sighed wanting so bad to come but not quite there yet. "I think I could manage," I said.

His teeth, shockingly white and perfect for a hillbilly (something I called him affectionately and then took my spanking like a good girl) clamped down on the side of my neck so that all the nerve endings sang out with pain and then a flash of sweet pleasure. He dropped his head, bit my nipple, thrust his fingers up high and hard, and I came like a dry twig snapping. It was fast and clean and brutal. Just the way he liked to make me come.

"So you'll come?" he asked. Smiling that smile of his. The smile of a man who gently demanded his way and got it. A subtle dictator. A secret king.

"I'll come," I said.

"Good girl." He worked his belt, dropped his jeans and grabbed my legs. "Better hold onto that bed post, Ellen. Here *I come*." He entered me with such ease it stole my breath. When my second orgasm curled through me, I begged him to kiss me.

Jared nodded and kissed me until my lips were bruised and I was ready for him all over again.

"Do you think your father will like me?"

"You want to meet him?"

"Wha...I...I mean I just assumed that—"

"I'm not sure you're ready to meet Daddy. He can be a bit..."

"Intimidating?"

"Larger than life."

"Okay," I said.

"Trust me. I just need to talk to him, but I want you to see the farm. I want you to see where I'm from."

"Cool." But I couldn't help feeling a bit of a letdown in my gut. A little hurt. An irrational urge to demand to meet a man I really wasn't ready to meet.

The farm was pretty. Way prettier than the prettiest park in the city. "I'll take you down by the creek to wait. There's a Weeping Willow down there planted by my great-great—"

"Whatever."

"Ellen."

"It's fine." I crossed my arms. What was I doing? I so *did not* want to meet his dad. The thought scared me to death. It was something I wanted whole-heartedly to avoid, and yet I opened my mouth and said, "I know you're ashamed of me."

He cut off the main road and the truck did a backwoods bump and grind over the field. I let out whoops and yelps like some heroine in a seventies car movie with guys who wore big moustaches and cowboy boots.

"Don't be ridiculous."

"It's fine. Fine!" I barked. "You...big. Dumb. Redneck!"

And that is how I found myself tied to the Weeping Willow tree by a picturesque creek. I fought my ties but Jared had done a good job. As usual. He'd crushed me up against the trunk, reaching his immense bulk around me and tied my arms with rope from the truck. Farm boys were like boy scouts, always prepared. In my ear he'd whispered a running monologue. "I'll deal with you when I get back, you brat. Temper tantrums are not acceptable. You should know better by now...think about that while I'm gone."

God help me the whole fucked up scenario had my panties damp and my heart slugging out an erratic tempo that had me light-headed. Jared had left me, growling "one for the road" and smacked me really hard on the ass cheek. Wet did not cover how I was between the legs.

I yanked hard and the rough rope bit into my wrists. Here came the panic, *how long would he be gone, did his father know, could anyone see me, I'd die out here alone on some rustic farm tied to a tree like a horror movie heroine while wild coyotes (were there coyotes around here?) feasted on my gorgeous tragic remains and...*

"Are you better behaved now, woman?" His hot breath was on my neck and I hadn't heard him coming. He lifted my little, silly city dress and tugged at my panties.

"Jared, I—"

"Hush up, now. No more bitching." His hands found me, and just as he slid two thick fingers home, he spanked my ass again. I yelped, I jumped, I went wetter for him.

"Your daddy..."

"My daddy was a big help." He left me there, panties down, dress bunched around my waist and walked to the end of one great swooping thin limb. The Weeping Willow had been a verdant umbrella of foliage hovering over me while he was gone. He took a buck knife and cut off a length. Then, as I watched, he stripped the tapered leaves free of the bark.

I swallowed hard. "What did he say?"

"He said that I should ask you to be my girl and maybe one day my wife if we had a handle on how things are between us."

His movements were casual as he sauntered to me. Jared tucked the willow switch under one arm and undid his jeans. His cock was flushed and ready and oh how I wanted him. But my eyes shot to that switch, and I shifted in place like I had to pee. I sighed.

"How are things?" I whispered.

"You were bad, and I need to punish you." I nodded.

"But don't you worry, honey. If you do good, I might reward you."

I nodded again.

It was six lashes for my mouth. Six lashes of impossibly

resilient green wood that bit at me like some small forest crea-
ture while I twisted in the wind, tied to the tree. Jared's girl
taking her punishment as Daddy suggested. Was this a family
trait I wondered. But only for an instant because the switch hit
the ground at my feet and he was in me. A swift thrust and my
Jared was seated deep. His fingers on my clit, his cock driving
into me.

"Do you take after your daddy, then?" I babbled, tears drying
on my cheeks. My cunt clutched up around him and I sighed.
Praying for the orgasm to come. Praying that it didn't.

He chuckled darkly. "Heh. Maybe."

Rough bark rubbed my face as he rocked against me, and
when my orgasm yanked me under, I heard him grunt. His own
release stealing his manners. My Jared, who this time had none
too gently demanded his way and gotten it. A subtle dictator. A
secret king.

ABOUT THE AUTHORS

XAVIER ACTON's work has appeared in Gothic.net, *Good Vibes Magazine,* and many anthologies, including *MASTER,* Violet Blue's *Sweet Life* series and *Taboo,* and various anthologies in the *Naughty Stories from A to Z* series. Acton lives in California, where he is at work on an erotic horror novel.

RACHEL KRAMER BUSSEL (www.rachelkramerbussel.com) is senior editor at *Penthouse Variations* and a contributing editor at *Penthouse* and writes the "Lusty Lady" column in the *Village Voice.* She is the editor of *Naughty Spanking Stories from A to Z* and *Cheeky: Essays on Spanking and Being Spanked* and coeditor of *Up All Night: Adventures in Lesbian Sex,* with several more dirty books on the way. Her writing has been published in over sixty erotic anthologies, including *Best American Erotica 2004,* as well as publications such as *AVN, Bust, Curve, Diva, Girlfriends,* Gothamist.com, *On Our Backs,* Oxygen.com,

Penthouse, Punk Planet, Rockrgrl, the *San Francisco Chronicle* and *Velvetpark.*

ERICA DUMAS's short erotica has appeared in the *Sweet Life* series, the *Naughty Stories* series, and numerous other anthologies. She lives with her lover in Southern California, where she is currently at work on a short story collection and an erotic novel. She can be contacted at ericamdumas@yahoo.com.

VANESSA EVANS isn't exactly a technophobe, but she does have a fondness for cassette tapes, videos, and phones with cords. Her work has appeared in *Penthouse Variations.*

C. D. FORMETTA was born in 1972. In Italy she has published *Il nero che fa tendenza.* Her stories regularly appear in *UP* magazine. Currently she's working on a comic strip for the publishing house Nicola Pesce Editore.

R. GAY wears many hats, one of which is that of writer. Her work can be found in *Best American Erotica 2004*, several editions of *Best Lesbian Erotica*, *Best Bisexual Women's Erotica*, *Best Transgender Erotica*, *The Mammoth Book of Tales from the Road*, and many others. She can be reached at rgay74@gmail.com.

SHANNA GERMAIN is a connoisseur of anything that can be put into her mouth: chocolate, beer, coffee, various body parts, silky fabrics, and nasturtiums. You can read more of her work in books like *Best Bondage Erotica*, *Heat Wave*, and *The Good Parts,* as well as on her website, www.shannagermain.com.

MICHAEL HEMMINGSON lives in San Diego, shuttling from Encinitas, Borrego Springs, and Ocean Beach. His most recent books are *Expelled from Eden: A William T. Vollmann Reader*; *In the Background Is a Walled City*; *The Las Vegas Quartet*; and *The Yacht People*.

MICHELLE HOUSTON has six ebooks out from Renaissance E Books, as well as a print omnibus of two of them, and stories in several anthologies, including *Heat Wave, Three-Way, Naughty Spanking Stories from A to Z Vols. 1* and *3*, and *Down & Dirty 2*. Michelle lives in the eastern United States with her husband and daughter. You can read more about her and see more of her writing on her personal website, The Erotic Pen (www.eroticpen.net). She loves to receive email, so drop her a line at thewriter@eroticpen.net.

DEBRA HYDE's fiction has appeared in several anthologies, most recently *Erotic Travel Tales 2*, *Best of the Best Meat Erotica*, and *Ripe Fruit: Erotica for Well-Seasoned Lovers*, with additional work scheduled to appear in several upcoming anthologies. She is a regular contributor to both *Scarlet Letters* (www.scarletletters.com) and *Yes Portal* (www.yesportal.com), and maintains the pansexual weblog, *Pursed Lips*.

MARILYN JAYE LEWIS's erotic short stories and novellas have been widely anthologized in the United States and Europe. Her erotic romance novels include *When Hearts Collide, In the Secret Hours*, and *When the Night Stood Still*. She is the editor of a number of erotic short story anthologies, including *Stirring Up a Storm*. Upcoming novels include *Twilight of the Immortal, Killing on Mercy Road*, and *Freak Parade*.

SOMMER MARSDEN is the author of *Hard Lessons, Dirty or Die, Calendar Girl, Lucky 13,* and *Base Nature*. Her work has appeared in dozens of erotica anthologies and numerous magazines. You can find out about what kind of trouble she's gotten herself into by visiting sommermarsden.blogspot.com. Knock first—she may be all tied up.

JULIA MOORE is the coauthor of the best-selling book *The Other Rules: Never Wear Panties on a First Date and Other Tips*, a spoof of the tragic dating guide *The Rules*. Her short stories have appeared in anthologies including *Sweet Life* and *Sweet Life 2, Naughty Stories from A to Z, Batteries Not Included*, and on the website www.goodvibes.com.

N. T. MORLEY is the author of more than a dozen published novels of dominance and submission, including *The Parlor, The Limousine, The Circle, The Nightclub, The Appointment,* and the trilogies *The Library, The Castle,* and *The Office*. Morley has also edited two anthologies, *MASTER* and *slave*.

The erotic fiction of **CHRISTOPHER PIERCE** has been published most recently in *Bound & Gagged, Men, Freshmen*; and *Honcho,* and in the anthologies *Ultimate Gay Erotica 2005, Naughty Spanking Stories from A to Z, Fratsex,* and *Friction 7: Best Gay Erotic Fiction*. Write to him at chris@christopherpierceerotica.com and visit his world online at www.ChristopherPierceErotica.com. He dedicates "Five Bucks a Swat" to Master Vincent.

JEAN ROBERTA teaches English in a Canadian prairie university and writes erotica, reviews, articles, and rants. Her stories have appeared in over twenty anthologies, including *Best Lesbian*

Erotica (2000, 2001, 2004, and 2005) and *Best Women's Erotica* (2000, 2003, 2005, and 2006). Her lesbian e-novel, *Prairie Gothic*, is available from Amatory Ink (www.amatory-ink.co.uk).

After a long career as a teacher and writer of a successful series of children's books, CATE ROBERTSON recently turned her attention to erotica. Her fiction has been published online at *Clean Sheets* and *Scarlet Letters*, as well as in several print anthologies. Cate lives in Canada with her husband.

THOMAS S. ROCHE's more than three hundred published short stories and three hundred published articles have appeared in a wide variety of magazines, anthologies, and websites. In addition, his ten published books include *His* and *Hers*, two books of erotica coauthored with Alison Tyler, as well as three volumes of the *Noirotica* series. He has recently taken up erotic photography, which he showcases at his website, www.skidroche.com.

MIA UNDERWOOD lives and works in the Fairfax region of Los Angeles.

SOPHIA VALENTI has a fondness for spinning kinky tales and a wicked addiction to coffee. She lives in New York City in an apartment with too many books and too few bookshelves. She often writes her naughty stories on a tiny laptop while riding the subway but has only once caught someone reading over her shoulder. Her erotic fiction has appeared in the Harlequin Spice anthologies *Alison's Wonderland* and *With This Ring I Thee Bed*, as well as several Pretty Things Press ebooks, including *Kiss My Ass*, *Cuffed*, *Bad Ass*, and *Torn*. Visit her at sophiavalenti.blogspot.com.

SASKIA WALKER is a British author who has had short erotic fiction published on both sides of the pond. You can find her work in *Seductions: Tales of Erotic Persuasion*; *Sugar and Spice*; *More Wicked Words* and *Wicked Words 5* and *8*; *Naughty Stories from A to Z Vol. 3*; *Naked Erotica*; *Taboo*; *Three-Way*; and *Sextopia*. She also writes erotic romance for Red Sage Publishing and her first novella, *Summer Lightning*, will be available soon. Please visit www.saskiawalker.co.uk for all the latest news.

ABOUT
THE EDITOR

Called a "literary siren" by Good Vibrations, **ALISON TYLER** is naughty and she knows it. She is author of a collection of short erotic fiction, *Exposed* (Cleis Press), and more than twenty-five explicit novels, including *Rumors, Tiffany Twisted,* and *With or Without You* (all published by Cheek), and the winner of "best kinky sex scene" as awarded by *Scarlet Magazine.* Her novels and short stories have been translated into Japanese, Dutch, German, Italian, Norwegian, Greek, and Spanish.

According to Clean Sheets, "Alison Tyler has introduced readers to some of the hottest contemporary erotica around." And she's done so through the editing of more than fifty sexy anthologies, including the erotic alphabet series (*A Is for Amour, B Is for Bondage, C Is for Coeds, D Is for Dress-Up...*), all published by Cleis Press, as well as the *Naughty Stories from A to Z* series, the *Down & Dirty* series, *Naked Erotica,* and *Juicy*

Erotica (all from Pretty Things Press). Please drop by www.
prettythingspress.com.

Ms. Tyler is loyal to coffee (black), lipstick (red), and tequila
(straight). She has tattoos but no piercings, a wicked tongue
but a quick smile, and bittersweet memories but no regrets. She
believes it won't rain if she doesn't bring an umbrella, prefers
hot and dry to cold and wet, and loves to spout her favorite
motto: "You can sleep when you're dead." She chooses Led
Zeppelin over the Beatles, the Cure over NIN, and the Stones
over everyone—yet although she appreciates good rock, she has
a pitiful weakness for eighties hair bands. In all things impor-
tant, she remains faithful to her partner of more than fifteen
years, but she still can't settle on one perfume.

Visit www.alisontyler.com for more luscious revelations or
myspace.com/alisontyler if you'd like to be her friend.